"What kind of business deal is so important that I had to meet with you today, Taylor?"

His question made her aware he was staring at her while waiting for her response. She swallowed. She couldn't get cold feet now. She was a risk taker and this would definitely be a risk worth taking.

"This *is* a business deal, but then it's also sort of personal."

She watched the lifting of his dark brow before he asked, "Personal? In what way?"

She paused for a second before she said, "I want to make you an offer that really won't cost you anything." *Just your sperm,* she decided not to add.

"Then what would be the investment on my part?" he asked. "And what will be the return?"

"The return is based on something I heard you say that every man should have a right to do."

"Which is?"

"To father a child."

Books by Brenda Jackson

Kimani Romance

Solid Soul
Night Heat
Beyond Temptation
Risky Pleasures
In Bed with Her Boss
Irresistible Forces

Kimani Arabesque

Tonight and Forever
A Valentine's Kiss
Whispered Promises
Eternally Yours
One Special Moment
Fire and Desire
Something to Celebrate
Secret Love
True Love
Surrender

BRENDA JACKSON

is a die "heart" romantic who married her childhood sweetheart and still proudly wears the "going steady" ring he gave her when she was fifteen. Because she's always believed in the power of love, Brenda's stories always have happy endings. In her real-life love story, Brenda and her husband of thirty-three years live in Jacksonville, Florida, and have two sons.

A *USA TODAY* bestselling author, Brenda divides her time between family, writing and working in management at a major insurance company. You may write to Brenda at P.O. Box 28267, Jacksonville, Florida 32226, e-mail her at WriterBJackson@aol.com or visit her Web site at www.brendajackson.net.

BRENDA JACKSON

IRRESISTIBLE FORCES

KIMANI™
ROMANCE

KIMANI PRESS™

ISBN-13: 978-0-373-86064-7
ISBN-10:   0-373-86064-1

IRRESISTIBLE FORCES

www.kimanipress.com

Printed in U.S.A.

Dear Reader,

In a very rare moment of sitting down and relaxing with the television on, I caught a segment of *Inside Edition* that told the story of a couple who booked a three-day getaway to an island where the hotel touts itself as a "way to enhance the baby-making process." In other words, this hotel actually has, on staff, experts who can help couples in the pursuit of getting pregnant. They're known as procreation vacations—a growing trend for couples who want to conceive—and they are offered by several Caribbean resorts.

Immediately, my mind went into that *what if* mode.

What if my couple—two intelligent and successful individuals—wanted a baby without the benefits of a relationship or marriage? And *what if* they took time out of their busy schedules and planned a weeklong procreation vacation?

I could just see the possibilities…and the sizzle and steam.

I hope you enjoy Taylor and Dominic's story as they embark on a week guaranteed to help them relax and focus on a "new" goal. The big question is, after their week is over, will the two want to return to their bachelor and bachelorette lifestyles?

Brenda Jackson

Chapter 1

A baby.

Taylor Steele's heart began beating rapidly the way it always did whenever she thought about her most ardent desire. A mixture of relief and anticipation soared through her upon realizing that she was about to embark upon a phase in her life that she had been looking forward to for a long time.

Motherhood.

She leaned back in the chair behind her desk and stared out the window while tapping her fingertips against her bottom lip. For the first time she wasn't appreciating the view of the Lincoln

Memorial. Her thoughts were on something else
entirely. She was inwardly counting her blessings.

During this past year she had achieved a number
of her goals. First by venturing out and starting up
her own wealth and asset management firm, which
she named Assets of Steele, and then moving from
New York to the nation's capital and purchasing a
beautiful condo with a view of the Potomac River
from her bedroom window. That wasn't at all bad
for a twenty-five-year-old woman who'd made the
decision after college not to return to her hometown
of Charlotte, North Carolina, and work for her
family's multimillion-dollar manufacturing company. Instead she had set her sights on New York
after accepting a position with one of the major
banks as a wealth and asset manager.

Now she could turn her attention to the final stage
of her plan that she needed in place before making
her most sought-after dream a reality. And that was
the man she had chosen to father her child without
the benefit of marriage. She was even open to joint
custody of the child, if he wanted to go that route.

A permanent hookup with someone was not
what she wanted, not even a teeny-tiny bit. Nor was
she looking for a long-term lover, either. A short-
term one could handle the task intended quite
nicely. The last thing she wanted was a long-term
romantic commitment of any kind.

But she was selective.

She had decided very early in her plans that not just any man would do. It had to be someone with all the qualities she wanted to pass on to her offspring. He had to be handsome, intelligent, caring, healthy and wealthy. Definitely wealthy; after all, wealth was her business. And with those "must-have" qualifications embedded deep in her mind, she could think of only one man who met her criteria.

Dominic Saxon.

She tried ignoring the warmth of sensations that seeped through her veins. Dominic was one of her clients and she had never met a man who radiated so much sensuality. Part African-American and part French, at thirty-four he was the epitome of every woman's fantasy and a major player in numerous women's nightly dreams. The sexiness was there in his looks, his body, when he walked, talked or just plain stared at you. He was definitely the most gorgeous man she'd ever encountered. Besides that, she knew from the many charities he was associated with that he was highly intelligent and caring. And although she wasn't privy to his health records, she had no reason to think he wasn't in the best of health and could not father a child. The man was as virile as any man could get.

From the very beginning she had been attracted to him and for the past two years it had taken everything she had to keep their relationship strictly business,

although he'd never given her the impression he
expected anything else. Whenever they met he was
always professional and courteous. She knew that he
merely saw her as one of his employees and nothing
more. He was paying a hefty fee for the services she
rendered and her job was to take all the wealth he'd
accumulated in his thirty-four years and make him
richer, which wasn't hard since he was an ace at
making the most of every financial opportunity.

It was common knowledge that he was the son
of a wealthy Frenchman and his beautiful African-
American wife, and from the time Dominic was
born he'd had the best of everything—schools,
social contacts and money, and he'd used all three
to his benefit. He rotated residences between the
United States and France, although she heard he
also owned a beautiful apartment in London, as well
as a private island off the French coast of Normandy.

Taylor picked up the brochure that had been sent
to her compliments of her youngest sister, Cheyenne.
It was meant to be a joke after a conversation the two
of them had shared a week ago when she'd told
Cheyenne that she wanted a baby, but not a husband.

Cheyenne had sent her the pamphlet that she'd
come across in her travels as a professional model
that advertised procreation vacations. *A week on a
Caribbean island, plenty of dirty talk with trained
professionals, exotic food and aphrodisiac-laden
drinks...and if needed, a week's supply of Viagra.*

It was advertised as a dream come true and the Bahamas resort encouraged potential guests to use their facilities for a week of near-constant, mind-blowing sex just for the purpose of making a baby. The packet Cheyenne had sent included several pictures bordering the brochure that could be considered X-rated. But they did a good job of getting their point across.

Compared to the frosty March weather they were experiencing, the island seemed like a really nice place to be right now. She could spend her time resting, relaxing and, of course, making a baby. Now if she could only convince the man she'd chosen to father her child to go along with her plan…

"Ms. Steele, Mr. Saxon has arrived."

Taylor's secretary's voice coming across the intercom interrupted her thoughts, and immediately she took a deep breath when more heady sensations coursed through her. It was time to put her plan into action. "Please escort him in, Mrs. Roberts."

Dominic Saxon checked his watch. He had just about an hour to meet with Taylor Steele and then he had an unexpected meeting back at the hotel. He had received a call from his parents saying they were flying into D.C. from California and wanted to meet with him. His father's voice had sounded urgent but he had refused to say what the meeting was about.

Whenever Dominic made a pit stop in the nation's

capital it was usually to check on the Saxon Hotel, just one of many his family owned in several major cities around the country. Usually Taylor would fly into New York for their meetings, so it came as a surprise when he'd gotten a call asking that he drop by her office on this trip.

She had been assigned as his financial advisor when she had worked for a bank in Manhattan. From the very beginning, the degree of her intelligence when it came to wealth management, as well as her comprehensive view of his personal portfolio, investment goals and financial objectives had amazed him. He was already a successful businessman but together they created a long-term strategy that was increasing his fortune exponentially.

Besides being very knowledgeable on financial affairs, he'd found Taylor to be an extremely beautiful woman. Even now he could recall the desire that had consumed him the first time he'd seen her and because of it, he had concluded the less he saw of his wealth and asset manager the better off he was. He had decided that first day that she was definitely a woman worth taking to his bed—he was one who didn't believe in mixing business with pleasure, no matter how enticing the thought or deep the craving. Yet the thought had remained lodged in his mind. He would be the first to admit it had been hard as hell to control the urge to take things further. He was used to beautiful women but there was something about Taylor Steele that caused him to think of hot sex every time he was in the same room with her.

Regardless of the iron-clad control he was known for—physically and emotionally—he was definitely a hot-blooded man, which was something he seemed to remember each and every time he breathed Taylor's scent.

"Ms. Steele is ready to see you, Mr. Saxon. I'll escort you in."

He stood and smiled at her secretary, a nice older lady, who seemed more suited to baking cookies for her grandkids than trying to tackle the huge computer sitting in front of her. "Thank you, and I don't need an escort."

"Yes, sir."

He fought for control of both his body and mind as he headed toward the door that had Taylor Steele's name plate on it.

Taylor inhaled a deep breath as she stared across the room at the man who walked into her office. He was wearing a black business suit with a white shirt that spelled out his wealth, and at thirty-four his mixed heritage made his looks striking. A sensuous shiver glided down her spine. He was simply gorgeous. His height, tall and imposing at six foot three, was hard to miss. She had seen photographs of him and his mother, a renowned fashion designer, earlier that year in *People* magazine. Megan Saxon was known for her beauty as well as for her skill and talent with fabrics.

From his mother, Dominic had inherited the shape of his lips, which could only be defined as full and sultry even on a male. He had his father's startling green eyes, which were a breathtaking contrast to his maple-brown coloring. Then there was the thick, black, curly hair that flowed past his shoulders when he wasn't wearing it back in a rakish-looking pony-tail…as he was now. And last but not at all least were the chiseled jaw, cleft chin and high cheekbones.

As she stared at him, her courage began wavering. Anyone would say she had a lot of nerve to propo-sition Dominic Saxon to father her child and then expect him to back off. But then anyone who thought she had a lot of nerve would know that in essence she really did. She was known to be gutsy enough to try anything once—as long as it was legal. And there was nothing illegal about making an offer. The only thing he could say was yes or no, and inwardly she crossed her fingers that she would get a yes.

What did she have to lose? A very profitable client was the first response that popped into her mind. Would he still want her to handle his financial affairs after she made such an outlandish request?

"Taylor?"

She let out a relaxed breath with the sound of her name from his lips. She loved his accent, a blend of

English and French. More than once during the course of their business meetings he would lapse into French without realizing he'd done so, and would quickly catch himself and revert back to English. She smiled. He hadn't yet figured out the fact that she also spoke French, not as fluently as he did but enough to get by. In fact she spoke several different languages, thanks to all those classes she'd taken while attending Georgetown. She had prepared herself to tap into the international markets.

"Dominic, I'm glad you were able to meet with me today." She liked the fact that they were on a first-name basis, a rule he had established the first time he had walked into her office as a new client. She also liked the fact that he had given her an appraisal from head to toe, which meant this new cobalt-blue business suit had made an impression. When she'd purchased it yesterday, she'd hoped that it would.

"No problem, but I do have an important meeting back at the hotel in a few hours, so my time with you will have to be brief," he informed her, breaking into her thoughts.

"I understand. Please have a seat," she said, coming from behind her desk.

He took the chair she offered and she sat in the one across from it, thinking it would be better not to sit behind her desk. Although she would be making what she considered a business proposition, she wanted less formality than usual.

"Thanks for seeing me on such short notice."

"No problem." What Dominic had said was true. It hadn't been a problem although he'd been surprised by her request to meet with him. She had moved from New York a few months ago, striking out on her own and leaving the company that had given her a start. Although her former employer had tried making a fuss, it had been Dominic's decision to follow Taylor, preferring to continue to do business strictly with her.

Today, as usual, she looked good. Because his mother was considered by many to be a fashion goddess, he appreciated anyone, man or woman, who displayed good taste in clothing. He considered himself, as well as his father, a fairly stylish dresser since Megan Saxon wouldn't have it any other way. He thought Taylor had great taste when it came to selecting her clothes. She was definitely a fashion-minded person who knew not only how to dress for success but also when to dress to impress. And he'd always been impressed each and every time he'd seen her.

And on top of that, she was a very attractive woman. Young, but attractive. Her dark brown hair was cut in a short and sassy style that was perfect for the oval shape of her face and her creamy cocoa-colored complexion. She was tall, leggy, with a curvy figure that enhanced the business suits she liked wearing.

When he'd first met her he'd thought someone at the bank was trying to pull a fast one over on him. There was no way a woman her age could handle the vast extent of his wealth. She had proven him wrong.

"How was your flight into the city?" she asked, reclaiming his thoughts.

"As usual Martin was excellent at the controls," he said of his private pilot. "It was good flying weather and he made the most of it."

Taylor nodded, trying not to stare at the way he was sitting in the chair—perfect posture, immaculately groomed and sexy to a fault.

"What kind of business deal have you put together that was so important you wanted us to meet today, Taylor?"

His question pulled her back in, made her aware he was staring at her while waiting for her response. She swallowed. She couldn't get cold feet now. She was a risk-taker and this would definitely be a risk worth taking.

"This *is* a business deal but then it's also sort of personal."

She watched the lifting of his dark brow before he asked, "Personal? In what way?"

She paused for a second before she said, "I want to make you an offer that really won't cost you anything." *Just your sperm,* she decided not to add.

He tilted his head slightly and gazed at her.

"Then what would be the investment on my part?" he asked. "And what will be the return?"

She was not surprised by his questions since the majority of their meetings always addressed investments and returns. "The return is based on something I heard you say that every man should have a right to do."

"Which is?"

"To father a child."

He frowned. "I don't recall ever saying anything like that to you."

She wouldn't expect him to remember. "It was last year, during the bank's Christmas party at Rockefeller Center. You made my boss extremely happy by making an appearance. One of the secretaries had dropped by and brought in her newborn baby for everyone to see. I believe you were speaking to yourself out loud more than making conversation with me."

His frown deepened as he continued to stare at her. "And just what did I say?"

"You were staring at the baby and said that every man should have a right to father a child and you regretted not having done so yet."

He nodded and she felt a rush of gratitude that he didn't deny having said such a thing. She shifted in her chair and met his gaze. "Is that true, Dominic? Is that something you regret not doing? Do you want a child?"

For the first time in their business relationship, she could feel his defense mechanism go up. He had often used it with others but never with her. And a part of her understood his need to use it now. He was a private person and she *was* asking him some rather personal questions.

"Why are we discussing this, Taylor?" he asked gruffly, narrowing his gaze at her.

Her emotions flinched at the look but she knew despite that, she had to go on. She paused a moment and then said, "We are discussing this because I feel the same way. I think every woman who wants a child should have the chance to mother one. And I want one."

The glare in his eyes indicated he wasn't quite following her, was still somewhat confused. "Then why don't you have one?" he asked flatly.

"I plan to do so…and that's why I've asked you here. It seems the two of us want the same thing and then again we don't want the same thing. We both want a child, but I've read you quoted many times as saying you will never marry again." She knew his wife had been killed in a car accident four years ago.

"Yes, and I was quoted correctly."

She nodded. "And getting married is the furthest thing from my mind, as well."

He leaned forward in his chair, holding her gaze under the penetrating stare of his green eyes. "Let's cut to the chase, shall we, Taylor. I still don't follow this business proposition of yours. You've established the fact that we both would like a child, but I don't know where that is leading."

She stood and picked up the brochure off her desk. "To this," she said, handing it to him. "You and I. Together. And a week spent on a procreation island in the Caribbean for the sole purpose of making a baby."

He looked at her as if she'd lost her mind as he accepted the brochure. He moved his gaze from her to the pamphlet. It took him a few moments to read it and then he lifted his head to meet her gaze again. "Aphrodisiac-laden drinks? Constant mind-blowing sex? Are you serious?"

She nodded nervously and grimaced when she heard the incredulity in his voice. Chances were he thought she had really lost it. "Yes," she replied, knowing she had to somehow convince him that she was still sane. "And I'd like to make you an offer. I want a baby, Dominic. Yours. A baby we will get to share. And to start things off we get to spend a week on that island. Many obstetricians even recommend such trips to couples who might find it difficult to conceive…not that I think we would have any problems. But it would take the tension off some and there is a guarantee of privacy. I've considered other options, such as having the procedure done by artificial insemination, however, I chose this route because I want my child conceived the normal way, a way I consider natural, with the two of us making love."

She inhaled deeply as he continued to stare at her. "Good heavens! Do you know what you're asking me?" he queried, his voice low and husky.

"Yes, trust me I know," she said, refusing to look away from the intensity of his stare. "But you are a man I have come to respect and admire and when I thought about a potential father for my child, I couldn't think of anyone else I would rather have. You have all the qualities that I want."

Dominic wasn't quite sure what to say to that, so instead he slowly got to his feet. The nature of this meeting was definitely a surprise to say the least. "There's no way I can decide on something such as this right this minute. We need to discuss your business proposition further and I suggest we do so tonight over dinner. Let's say around seven o'clock at the hotel. Is that time okay?"

She swallowed. At least he hadn't given her a flat-out no. "Yes, that's fine."

"Good. I'll send my driver for you around six-thirty. My secretary will contact you later today for an address."

"All right."

He walked toward the door and before reaching it, he turned back around and said, "I'll see you tonight, Taylor."

He stared at her for a moment longer and then

she watched as he turned and walked out of her office. It was only after he left she realized he had taken the brochure with him.

The driver opened the door and Dominic slid onto the plush leather seats of the limo. "Where to, Nick?"

"Back to the hotel, Ryder."

When the car began moving Dominic glanced down at the brochure he still held in his hand as his mind recalled everything Taylor had said. The brochure was proof he hadn't imagined it. She wanted a baby. His baby. And she wanted them to spend a week on some island in the Caribbean to make it happen. To say he was stunned would be an understatement, but he had heard the sincerity in Taylor's voice. She was dead serious.

He began reading the piece of literature. If the words didn't hit him below the gut, the pictures most definitely did. Procreation vacations. Just when he thought he'd heard it all. Evidently not. According to the brochure, it was a growing trend for couples that wanted to conceive. And Taylor Steele wanted to conceive.

If he were totally honest with himself, he would admit that so did he. The thought had crossed his mind several times in the past year, ever since his father's bout with prostate cancer last year. Thanks to early detection, surgery hadn't been needed and there were only short-term side effects.

His father's condition had made Dominic realize two things. His parents weren't the invincible couple he'd always assumed them to be. And although they both appeared to be in great physical shape, nonetheless, they were aging with each passing day.

Another thing he had come to realize, although they'd never mentioned it, was that his parents longed for a grandchild. He saw it in their eyes each and every time any of their friends talked about their grandchildren. There was no doubt in his mind if Camry had lived they would have had a child or two by now. But she hadn't lived and for the past four years he had somehow managed to go on, with the beautiful memories they'd shared to sustain him.

His parents had understood that after Camry's death the thought of ever marrying again was as foreign to him as life on another planet. Without realizing she had done so, Taylor may have provided him with the very solution to a problem that had been bothering him for some time.

He resumed reading the brochure. The success rate of the woman returning from one of these trips pregnant was very high but what intrigued him the most was the mere thought of checking into a resort with Taylor with the sole intent of having a full week of constant sex. He was getting aroused just thinking about it, about the possibility of making all those fantasies he'd tried pushing to the back of his mind about Taylor a reality.

But still, all things considered, he and Taylor would need to discuss the issue more in detail. There were a number of questions he needed answered, such as what joint custody of a child they shared would entail, and why did she think him making her pregnant would not cost him anything? Did she expect him to walk away from any financial obligations he had toward the child?

He settled back in the cushions of the seat thinking he was very much looking forward to his dinner date with Taylor later tonight.

"Your parents are waiting for you in your suite, Mr. Saxon."

Thanks, Harold," Dominic said to the hotel manager moments before crossing the huge lobby to the bank of elevators that would carry him up to the penthouse. The Saxon Grand was a beautiful hotel and had been the first Saxon Hotel. It was built twenty-five years ago and Dominic was almost certain Harold was hired in some position at that time, which would make him one of Saxon Hotel's oldest employees. And Harold was good at what he did, based on the customer satisfaction surveys that were periodically done. Customers visiting the area kept coming back knowing they would receive first-class service.

Moments later Dominic walked into his suite unannounced to find his parents in a loving embrace.

He was not surprised nor the least embarrassed to see them standing in the middle of the floor sharing a passionate kiss. Despite having been married for thirty-six years, Marcello and Megan were still deeply in love. That was obvious to anyone around them for any length of time. As long as he could remember, his parents were openly affectionate. He'd always known how much they loved each other as well as how much they had unselfishly loved him.

He cleared his throat to let them know of his presence. "Mom and Dad, it's good seeing you," he said, and knew he didn't have to add that it was also good seeing they were still very much in love.

His parents had met when Marcello Saxon had arrived in the United States from France to attend Yale. In his senior year he met the beautiful and vivacious Megan Spectrum and they fell in love immediately. It hadn't mattered that he was French and she African-American. What had mattered was the love they had for each other. They had gone so far as to defy Marcello's father, who'd threatened to disown his son—the heir to the Saxon wealth—if a marriage took place. Choosing love over wealth, Marcello had married Megan a year later and good to his word, Franco Saxon had practically disowned his son, had barely spoken to him since and only recently had acknowledged the marriage.

Dominic saw the worried look in his father's gaze. "What's wrong, Dad?" His father had recently

had his annual checkup and Dominic inwardly
prayed there wasn't bad news in that regard.

Marcello read the concern in his son's gaze and
said, "No, I'm fine. The doctors gave me another
clean bill of health after my last checkup. But we
did get some news last night that your grandfather
has taken ill."

Dominic stared first at his father and then at his
mother. Finally he shrugged nonchalantly as he
crossed the room to give his father a bear hug.
"Have you forgotten, Father, that I don't have a
grandfather?"

"Nick," his father said in a frustrating tone, "how
can you be so unforgiving?"

Dominic arched a brow. "And how can you be so
forgiving? That man refused to accept my mother
as your wife, publicly denounced your marriage
and you, didn't speak to you for years, never
acknowledged my birth and then out of the clear
blue sky last year when he'd heard you had taken
ill, he showed up and expected everyone to kiss and
make up. Well, I wasn't in the kissing mood then
and I'm not in it now," he said in an angry tone.

He switched his gaze from his father to smile down
at his mother. "Except for this beautiful woman here,"
he said, before hugging her close and placing a soft
kiss across her cheek. "How are you, Mama?"

Megan Saxon returned her son's smile before
giving him a scolding look. "I'm fine, Nick, and

your father is right, you know. You can't distance your grandfather forever."

"Would you care to bet on that?"

She frowned. "You're just like your father. Stubborn."

A smile touched Dominic's lips. "Yet you love us anyway."

Dominic then glanced at the man who'd sired him. The man he loved, admired and respected above all else. The man who had not let his father's rejection of the woman he loved destroy his determination to make her his wife and to make something out of his life—even without the Saxon wealth behind him. After college Marcello had started from the bottom and with keen intelligence, his father built his own Saxon empire, which consisted of hotels, cruise liners, restaurants, publishing companies and various auto dealerships across the country.

His mother hadn't done badly, either, he thought with a proud smile. Megan Saxon's name was known throughout the world and graced the garments of several international celebrities. She had a remarkable reputation for outstanding design and had established her own empire in the world of fashion.

The one thing his parents had taught him, Dominic concluded, was to increase his own wealth and not depend on what he might or might not inherit. And so he had. With their blessings he had carved out his personal legacy and thanks to a sharp wealth asset manager like Taylor, he was doing quite well for himself.

Taylor.

He glanced at his watch. They would be sharing dinner in less than four hours.

"Regardless of what you say or how you feel, Nick, he is still your grandfather."

Dominic decided not to justify his father's statement with a response.

"Will you at least think about going to see him, sweetheart?"

That question came from his mother. He glanced down at her. She was five feet, eight inches tall and in a room with her son and husband she looked small and delicate. But he knew the latter was far from the truth. She had to be one of the most headstrong women that he knew, definitely no pushover.

It was on the tip of his tongue to say there was nothing to think about and that under no circumstances did he intend to go see the man, but the last thing he wanted was to upset his mother any further. It bothered her that he disliked his grandfather so much because of the old man's treatment of her.

"I'll think about it," he said, although he knew deep down that he wouldn't.

"And that's all we ask you to do, Nick," his mother said softly. "We're staying in the suite across the hall tonight and flying to France in the morning."

He nodded. If they expected him to drop everything and fly to France with them because the old man had taken ill then they were wrong. He leaned over and swept another kiss across his mother's cheek. "And I hope the two of you have a safe flight."

He saw the flash of disappointment in her eyes and chose to ignore it. "Now if the two of you will excuse me I have a few things I need to take care of before my date tonight here in my suite."

His mother's brow lifted in surprise. "You have a date?"

He smiled. His mother was well aware that he rarely entertained anyone in a place he considered his private domain. "Yes. But don't waste the excitement. I'm merely meeting with my financial advisor."

"Oh."

He chuckled. "The two of you can join us if you like," he invited, knowing they wouldn't.

"Your mother and I have other plans," his father said, smiling and gently pulling Megan out of Dominic's arms into his and kissing her lips. "We're having dinner with friends."

"Okay then. Enjoy yourselves." And then Dominic's thoughts immediately went back to Taylor and her outlandish proposition. He glanced at his watch again. He couldn't wait to see her later.

Chapter 2

"Do you really think he's going to go along with it, Taylor?"

Taylor heard the uncertainty in her sister's voice through the phone. Vanessa was the one with doubts; however, Cheyenne was the sister who was convinced Dominic would accept her offer. And it wasn't that Vanessa was a naysayer. She was just being realistic that most people thought logically. And what Taylor was posing to Dominic was highly illogical.

The three of them, she, Vanessa and Cheyenne, always had a close relationship growing up and over the years that hadn't changed. Vanessa, the oldest at twenty-seven, was the one who, after getting a grad degree at Tennessee State, had returned to Charlotte to work at the family's manufacturing business, The Steele Corporation, along with their four older male cousins—Chance, Sebastian, Morgan and Donovan. After college, Taylor and Cheyenne had chosen to seek opportunities far away from North Carolina. Cheyenne, who was twenty-three, was a professional model and that meant a lot of traveling as well as living in some of the most exotic places in the world.

Vanessa was in the midst of planning a June wedding to a very handsome man by the name of Cameron Cody. Taylor couldn't help but smile when she thought about how Cameron had pursued her sister with a vengeance, and finally succeeded in capturing Vanessa's heart. Taylor was happy for Vanessa and looked forward to returning home for a brief stay this weekend to be fitted for her bridesmaid dress.

"Taylor?"

Vanessa didn't have to repeat the question for Taylor to respond. She knew what Vanessa wanted to know. "Um, I don't know if Dominic will go along with my offer or not. It would certainly make my day if he did. At least I'll have another chance to convince him that I haven't lost my mind at dinner tonight."

"Well, good luck."

"Thanks, Vanessa." Deciding to change the sub-

ject, she said, "So tell me how the plans are coming
for the wedding."

An hour or so later, Taylor was stepping out of
the shower to get dressed for her dinner meeting
with Dominic. His secretary had called earlier to get
her address and to let her know that a car was being
sent to pick her up exactly at six-thirty. She would
be taken to the Saxon Grand Hotel, where she
would be dining with Mr. Saxon.

Taylor glanced at the outfit and accessories she
had placed on the bed earlier. She would be wearing
a mauve embroidered overlay dress with gold covair
beading on the empire bodice and a hem that
stopped well above the knee to show off her legs.
The dress wasn't flashy, but she had to admit it was
eye-catching. Deliberately so. She needed an outfit
that would make Dominic take notice and quickly
conclude that a week spent with her on a tropical
island indulging in unlimited bedroom activities
wouldn't be all bad.

With less than thirty minutes before the car was
to arrive, Taylor was standing in front of the mirror
in her bedroom studying the finished product. She
tilted her head back, liking the way the earrings
dangled from her ears and the matching necklace
around her neck. Both had been Christmas gifts
from her oldest cousin, Chance, and his wife, Kylie.

Taylor still found it hard to believe at times that
within a three-year period her staunch bachelor

cousins, Chance, Sebastian and Morgan, had fallen in love and gotten married. And then there was Vanessa, who would be marrying Cameron in June. Taylor was happy for all four of them. Her thoughts shifted to the one lone single male cousin, Donovan Steele. At thirty-two, marriage was the furthest thing from his mind. She had even heard him swear that he would be a bachelor for life.

Her sister Cheyenne was pretty much like her—too involved in a career to take the time to settle down and get involved in a serious affair. But Taylor was determined that no matter how involved she was in her career, she would take time out to become a mother. Having a child had always been her lifelong desire, but she hadn't known to what degree until a few months back when she returned home to attend Morgan's celebration party, after he won the council-at-large seat in Charlotte, becoming the first Steele to enter politics.

Vanessa's best friend, Sienna, had just given birth to a little boy, who in keeping with Bradford tradition had been named Dane William Bradford IV. The moment Taylor had held Little Dane in her arms she'd known that she didn't want to wait any longer to become a mom.

Sighing deeply, Taylor glanced at her watch. Dominic's driver would be arriving to pick her up any moment and she wanted to be ready. When she saw Dominic again, she definitely wanted to give

him a few things to think about. He would discover
tonight that she was a lot more than a mover and a
shaker. She was a woman who went after what
she wanted and more than anything, she wanted
Dominic Saxon as her baby's daddy.

Dominic glanced at his watch periodically as he
paced around his hotel room waiting for Taylor's
arrival. He couldn't recall the last time a dinner date
had him on edge.

Earlier, during a relaxing moment, he had shared
a glass of wine with his parents, and as always, he
had enjoyed their company. They didn't always see
eye to eye on everything but he couldn't ask for
better parents. They had always been there for him,
supportive in every way.

He couldn't help noticing how worried his father
was about Franco Saxon's health. It had taken
Marcello years to finally put the anger behind him
and accept the olive branch that Franco had held out
after over thirty years. Dominic hadn't been that forgiving and to this day he had come face-to-face
with the man who was his grandfather only twice.
The most recent time was the day Franco had flown
in from Paris and had shown up at Dominic's
parents' home in Los Angeles after getting word that
his only son—the one he had years ago disowned—
had a life-threatening illness. Luckily, Marcello's
condition hadn't been as bad as all that, but it had

reunited father and son. Marcello was of the mind that too much hurt and pain had passed and as long as Franco finally accepted his marriage, all was well. Before he had left to return to France, Franco had given his blessings to the marriage.

Dominic frowned. As far as he was concerned it had come years too late and he had told the old man as much. But it seemed Dominic's words had fallen on deaf ears since Franco had refused to give up, determined to forge a bond with his only grand-child. Dominic had repeatedly turned down his grandfather's attempts. A part of him could not put aside the deep animosity he felt and move on.

Before taking a shower he had touched base with his kitchen staff. Dinner would be served here in his suite, which was a first for him. He rarely brought company to his hotel room, but given the topic of his and Taylor's conversation, it was important that whatever was discussed was done in private.

Hours later, after getting dressed, he paused to think about everything he knew about Taylor.

He knew from past conversations with her that her mother was still alive but that her father had died years back of lung cancer. He also knew she had two sisters and she was the middle child. And he was well aware that her family owned a multimillion-dollar business, The Steele Corporation, where she had a seat on the board of directors. He knew Chance Steele, her cousin, who was the CEO of the company. They had met years ago at a business conference and Dominic found him to be a very likable person.

Dominic also was acquainted with Cameron Cody, the man her oldest sister would be marrying. They moved in the same social circles and had even been involved in a highly successful business venture a few years back. When it came to business Cody was sharp as a tack.

Dominic wondered if Taylor's family was aware of how she intended to branch into motherhood. She wanted a baby, but not a husband. All things considered, he could certainly entertain the thought of having a baby without a wife. However, before he agreed to Taylor's proposal there were a number of things he had to think about, questions he needed answered.

On the flip side, he definitely had no qualms about accepting her proposal. He was attracted to her and had been from the first. Making a baby with her would definitely give him the excuse he needed to cross over the line of business only. The thought of having Taylor in bed beneath him while making love to her had kept him aroused all day.

The phone rang and he was jerked out of his thoughts. He quickly moved across the room to pick it up. "Yes?"

"Your guest has arrived, sir. Do you want me to escort her up?"

"No, I'll be down to meet her myself."

He hung up the phone feeling, oddly, a bit nervous.

Taylor glanced around thinking that this was the first time she had been in a Saxon Hotel. It was big and spacious with an understated degree of refined elegance. It was definitely a five-star that was replete with a luxurious-looking grand interior and a uniformed staff on duty to satisfy a client's every whim. A person could definitely get swept away with such grace and style.

"Mr. Saxon will be coming down for you, Ms. Steele."

Taylor glanced at the uniformed man who had spoken. He was the same one who had picked her up from her condo and now stood solidly beside her. "He is?"

"Yes."

She figured once inside the hotel she would be on her own. Apparently not. It appeared Dominic had other ideas. When he had invited her to dinner she'd known they would be dining in his suite. He hadn't said as much but she had assumed it. He was a private person and the majority of the time when they had dinner meetings he always made it a habit to suggest a private room. It wasn't uncommon for him to cause a stir, especially among the media who enjoyed writing about the wealthy Saxon heir.

"Here is Mr. Saxon now."

Taylor glanced in the direction of the elevators and caught sight of Dominic walking toward them. She had prepared herself to see him again. Or so she thought. The man was so extraordinarily sexy, so ridiculously sensual that her entire body began responding. As he crossed the wide stretch of lobby toward her, people, mainly women, stopped to stare.

She suddenly felt her heart take a nosedive into her stomach. He was wearing a tailored suit and blue shirt that fit him with precision and even at a distance she could detect his calm restraint. She was about to look away and place her focus else-where, when his gaze suddenly snagged hers. His penetrating stare was doing things to her, forcing her to embark on one hell of a fantastic voyage. Heat rushed through her, zinged her with a force she hadn't felt before. The man had enough sex appeal to bottle for future generations.

Damn. Definitely not what she wanted to be up against tonight. How was she going to get through a meal with him when already she felt trapped in his gaze? *All right, I can handle this. I can handle him.* Those words flowed through her mind as he got closer. With a half smile she expelled another breath and forced back the thought that suddenly entered her mind about just how great it would be to share a hotel room with him, a bed, the same intimate space. Hot sex. Heated Sex. Never-ending Sex. And all for a full week. With her lips barely moving, she released a soft laugh. There would be little time for chitchat.

That thought put every nerve ending in her body on red alert. But she refused to give anything away. So she stood there waiting, looking more poised than she actually felt. She was here for a good reason and knowing that reason gave strength to her resolve. It would be pointless to fight off the sexual heat the man generated but she wished she wasn't so aware of him. She would have appreciated it if he didn't make such a powerful impact on her vital signs and wasn't oozing such raw physical force.

And more than anything, she wished he didn't look like all the millions he was actually worth. Boy, how she wished.

When he finally came to a stop in front of her, and she saw the beauty of his green eyes as he gazed into her dark ones, she had never wished for anything so much in her life.

The first thing that had hit Dominic, even before he'd reached Taylor, was her scent. He had to compliment whatever perfume she was wearing. It was both soft and sensuous and had a punch that could drive a man to distraction. But then he had been blown away the moment he had stepped off the elevator and had seen her standing with Ryder. She looked delicate beside the huge hulk of man. Above all, she looked stunning.

The dress she was wearing definitely brought out her sensual side. Thanks to his mother he knew enough about fashion to realize that not every woman would be able to pull off wearing an outfit such as this. You had to have the small waistline, curves and legs to make it happen, otherwise it would be a total waste of good fabric. Taylor had the small waistline, the curves and the legs. Another added bonus was that she also had the breasts, since the square-neck bodice emphasized them. Yes, altogether he would give the outfit an A-plus.

Even now as he stared at her, with her head tilted and meeting his intense gaze, he was fighting for control. He had always admired Taylor for her intelligence, her investment savvy, but now he was about to bestow on her accolades for her ability to take him on at a personal level. He was beginning to discover that she was one irresistible force.

"Dominic."

His name on her lips seemed to warm his skin. He even felt his insides beginning to melt. He figured he needed to get her up to his hotel room before his sexual response to her became too obvious. "Taylor, I hope you had a pleasant ride coming here."

She smiled as she glanced over at Ryder. "Um, it was rather interesting."

Only someone who knew Ryder Sanders as well as Dominic was aware of the man fighting the urge to smile back. Evidently his driver had broken several speed limits.

Years ago, when at the age of fourteen, a kidnapping attempt had been made on Dominic, Franco Saxon, in one of his rare but manipulative moves had sent Ryder. Marcello had been too distraught at the thought of someone trying to use his son in a ransom scheme to send Ryder back. By the time Dominic had learned of his grandfather's gesture, Ryder had become not only his bodyguard, driver and traveling companion, but the now fifty-something man had become his good friend. Dominic moved around freely knowing that Ryder had his back.

"Interesting?" Dominic said. "I'm sure it was. Are you ready to go up to my suite for dinner?"

"Yes, I'm ready."

The sound of her voice stoked the fires within him once again. There was a whole world of difference between the Taylor he met each month to discuss his financial portfolio and the one standing in front of him looking good enough to devour. All of a sudden the menu that he'd carefully selected lost its appeal and he was developing a taste for something else altogether. Something that was just as succulent.

He gestured toward the bank of elevators. "There's a private one that goes up to the floor where the owner suites are located."

She began walking beside him across the lobby floor. He saw several heads turn and knew everyone was probably thinking they made a beautiful couple. Little did they know that during the course of the next few hours they would be encased in his hotel room discussing whether or not they should make a beautiful baby together.

His heart began to thunder in his chest. He had a feeling it would be a long and tempting evening.

This had to be the longest elevator ride that she'd ever taken, Taylor thought as she tried looking at everything other than Dominic. He was standing beside her and she felt tension grip her stomach.

She didn't feel like engaging in a nice conversation just to pass the time. Although she and Dominic had spent many hours together poring over his financial portfolio, their meeting tonight would be altogether different. She was now a woman with a plan. And it was a plan that she hoped he would go along with.

"I should have asked before commissioning the cook to come up with something special for dinner tonight if you're allergic to anything."

She glanced up at him. "No, there's nothing I can think of that doesn't agree with my system."

"I'm glad to hear that."

She met his eyes. They were staring deep into hers.

"And don't be surprised if we see my parents at some point tonight."

She arched a brow. "Your parents?"

"Yes. They're here at the hotel. They flew in from California and are on their way out of the country."

She nodded. "I've seen pictures of them together in various magazines. They make a nice couple," she said, meaning every word. Marcello Saxon was an extremely handsome man with his classic French looks. And Dominic's mom was a beauty, who didn't look a day past forty. In a rare photo that Dominic and his parents had taken together that had appeared in *People* magazine earlier this year, Megan Saxon looked young enough to have passed for his sister.

"Thanks, and I agree. They do make a nice couple. I am fortunate to have them as parents."

The elevator came to a stop and the doors swooshed open. Dominic stood back for her to walk out ahead of him and then he was there again, by her side, leading the way down an elegantly carpeted hall toward a set of double doors at the end.

They came to a stop at the doors. "The kitchen staff was arriving when I was leaving so everything should be set up now," he was saying. "We can discuss things over dinner and, if need be, converse further afterward."

As she stared into his green eyes she suddenly felt a heated rush, a swamp of sensations of the strongest kind. It was nothing more than a business meeting over dinner, yet she had to get Dominic to see how useful they could be to each other, how together they could bring something or rather someone special into each of their lives.

As he opened the door to his penthouse she knew she was about to have her one shot at it and she didn't intend to blow it.

"So, Taylor, when did you come up with the idea of wanting me to father your child?"

Dominic watched as she took a deep breath before raising her eyes from her plate to look at him. He had caught her off guard. She hadn't been expecting his question, especially not now. They were in the midst of enjoying a delicious and impressive entrée the hotel's restaurant had prepared and had been discussing a recent documentary that had aired on television that focused on the plight of finback whales. He had discovered a while back that they were both lovers of sea life.

She put her fork down beside her plate. "I made the decision once I knew I wanted to move ahead with my plans to become a mother."

He lifted his hand in the briefest gesture before asking, "And? What were your other options?"

"I had several," she said, leaning back in her chair. Anyone observing would assume she was rather comfortable with their conversation, but he had a feeling she really wasn't.

"I could have contacted a sperm bank where the identity of my child's father would never be known by me or by him or her. Or I could have engaged in a one-night stand for the sole purpose of getting pregnant. Neither appealed to me."

"But I did."

"Yes, you did," she answered in what he thought was a polite tone. "You had all the characteristics I looked for in a man and those I want to pass on to my son or daughter, as well."

He didn't say anything for a moment and then, "And you were sure I wanted a child?"

"Yes, after the night of the Christmas party, I was sure. Although there was the question of whether you would be interested in doing what I was proposing. For all I know you might already have a woman selected as the mother of your child."

He took a sip of his wine, thinking that he didn't. In fact he had pretty much dropped the thought from his mind. He figured that there were a number of women who would love the opportunity to mother his child—most of them were gold diggers and would use the child to keep a tight rein on him and his finances.

"If I decide to go along with what you're proposing I know what I'll be bringing to the table, Taylor. What will you bring?"

Again his question had caught her off guard. He knew what she would bring to the bedroom—that was a given. Sitting across from her, inhaling her scent while visions of all the things they would be doing together on that island ran through his mind was playing havoc with certain body parts. She was fully dressed now, but he could see her naked while he made love to her, day in and day out. She was temptation at its finest and the thought that he wouldn't have to resist temptation for an entire week had his body throbbing.

"I'll bring to the table the assurance that your child will be loved and well cared for. I consider myself intelligent, motivated and financially secure."

"What about custody?" he asked.

She frowned slightly. "I'm open to joint custody."

"So you won't have a problem with me being a part of my child's life?"

She shook her head. "No. I'm not one of those women who believes a child doesn't need a male presence in its life. I have four male cousins who I'm close to, but still, I'd want my child's father to be a part of its life if possible."

Dominic absorbed her words while his gaze settled impassively on his wineglass. He then lifted his gaze to her. "And just what will our relationship be? After our visit to that island?"

"If I get pregnant…" She paused then corrected the sentence by saying, "*After* I get pregnant, then our relationship will become that of expectant parents and not lovers. The job at that point would have been done. Of course, I'm hoping that I will continue to be your wealth and asset manager."

He thought she didn't have to worry about that unless the island rendezvous turned into an absolute fiasco. He was one who normally didn't mix business with pleasure, yet if he agreed to her proposal he would be doing just that. But she was right. He had on several occasions entertained the thought of having a child without having to deal with a wife. Since his wife's death he'd dated but hadn't yet met a woman he wanted to share his name again.

He and Camry had been childhood sweethearts, their parents the best of friends. It had seemed natural for them to eventually marry. In a way they had been best friends instead of two people who were deeply in love with each other. They'd shared a close relationship. He could talk to Camry about anything and she had understood him better than anyone. She had been his confidante as well as his wife. He doubted he would find such closeness with another woman. And to be honest, he wasn't interested in doing so ever again.

"You seem certain that you will get pregnant," he said, inwardly smiling to himself and thinking he was just as certain she would get pregnant. He wanted her and as far as he was concerned that said it all. Heat had been running through every part of his body since she had arrived. It wasn't easy now sharing table space with her.

"I don't have any reason to think that I won't, given the planned agenda," she said. "I've been under a doctor's supervision for the past three months. I've been tracking my basal body temperature, which will help me to pinpoint the best time to conceive and that's the week I want us on that island."

"In that case why go to the island? Why not stay here?"

"I prefer the island. It will provide a more relaxed environment."

He had to agree with that. "And you have no problem sleeping with me for no other reason than to make a baby?"

He watched her lips curve into an assured smile. "No, I don't have a problem with it." She fell silent for a moment then asked, "Do you?"

He thought about her question. He would be breaking rules he'd put in place for specific reasons, rules he'd always enforced when it came to his business relationships. When it came to women, period. Although he was not suspicious regarding her motives for what she wanted to do, he still wasn't a hundred percent certain it was what he wanted to do.

"What if we aren't compatible, Taylor?"

"Excuse me?"

His mouth formed into a smile. Apparently she found the idea absurd. "I said what if we aren't compatible? How do we know we're even attracted to each other? That we'll be able to click?"

She chuckled softly. "Trust me. We'll be able to click."

"How do you know?"

"Because I do."

"Prove it."

One of the first things he had discovered about Taylor was that she liked challenges, which was one of the reasons she was successful at what she did. However, he could tell from her present expression that proving what he'd suggested was the last thing she wanted to do. Still, not one to forgo an opportunity to prove him wrong, she released a long, slow breath as she stood. He then watched as she walked around the table until she came to a stop beside him. Reaching out, she touched his hand and the impact of that touch for some reason almost took his breath away. He then tossed his napkin aside, slid his chair back and got to his feet to face her.

"Not that I'm an expert on sexual chemistry or anything," she said in a low, sultry tone. "But I think this will eliminate any doubt in your mind on whether or not we will click."

She reached up on tiptoe, placed her arms around his neck and brought her mouth to his. His heart pounded hard in his chest the moment their lips touched. And when their tongues began mating with an intensity that shook every nerve in his body, he had to fight the urge to break the connection for fear of losing control. At that moment he wasn't aware of anything but the feel of his tongue stroking hers, the feel of hers stroking his, the rush of sensations flooding and overpowering him. He was also aware of the fire stirring in his loins and of the way his body was beginning to ache.

When she slowly pulled back, their lips reluctantly separating, he felt a tremendous sense of loss. "So," she said slowly, dragging the word out softly as she eased away from his lips. "Did we click?"

He struggled to free his mind, as well as the tight squeeze on certain body parts as he studied her. He saw her lips that had been thoroughly kissed, lips that had to be the sweetest pair that he'd ever tasted, sampled, devoured. His response to her was as potent as any intoxicating drink he'd ever taken. And from the heated look in her eyes, she was just as affected by the kiss as he was.

"Yes," he finally said, pulling in a deep, hot breath. "I can say with all certainty that we click."

Chapter 3

Taylor stood at the window that had the Jefferson Memorial as a backdrop as she thought about the kiss she and Dominic had shared. Lucky for her a slight reprieve had come when his cell phone rang and he'd excused himself to take the call in private.

She refused to believe that she had bitten off more than she could chew. She had known from the beginning that Dominic was the epitome of a sexy male, a challenge to any woman's hormones and a mass of French-American testosterone all rolled into one. At the time she had decided she wanted him as the father of her child, there was no doubt in her mind that she could handle him. What she hadn't done was take the time to consider all of the consequences.

She traced her lips with her tongue, still tasting him there. She hadn't counted on not being in control of any situation with him, but if that kiss had lasted any longer than it had, she would have lost control. Completely. She had been kissed before, several times, but she had never considered or remembered the occasions as being the highlight of her life. One kiss was the same as another. Mouths connecting. Lips tasting. Tongues playing.

But what she had shared moments ago with Dominic was all those things and more. She hadn't counted on the rush of desire that had radiated through every part of her body at the same time that her insides began a slow meltdown under intense heat. She wished she could claim her reaction had been the result of restless energy being tapped or the release of bottled-up sexual tension. What Dominic had done was place an all-out assault on her senses, each one of them, and it would take her some time to recover from the tingling rush of desire she still felt. It was desire of a magnitude that had never invaded her body before. Even now she could imagine his hands on her, stroking her naked skin, his lips tasting every inch of her willing body and their bodies connecting in the most primitive way known to man. There was no doubt in her mind that when and if they shared a bed they would literally burn up the sheets.

"Sorry about the interruption."

She slowly turned around. He might have been sorry about it, but she had welcomed it. It had given her time to pull herself together or at least try to. "No need to apologize. You're a businessman who works 24-7." She smiled. "As your asset manager I can certainly appreciate that."

Her eyes roamed over him, liking the way his muscles filled out the suit he was wearing. There were a number of other things she could appreciate at that moment but decided it would be safer not to think about them right now.

When he stood there staring at her without saying anything, she felt a bit cornered, placed under his personal microscope, and she couldn't help wondering what he was thinking. So she decided to ask. "You seem absorbed in some intense thought, Dominic. What are you thinking?"

A smile stretched his lips as he crossed the room to her. And when he reached out and ran the back of his hand along her cheek, the throbbing between her legs intensified. "I was more envisioning than thinking," he finally said in a deep, husky tone. "I was trying to picture in my mind you pregnant with my child."

Taylor bit her lip. He should have said anything but that. She knew at that moment her fate was sealed. He had made a decision or was close to making one. And although what they would agree to do would be illogical, definitely outlandish to some people, to her it would be absolutely incredible, a dream come true.

"Does that mean you've made a decision, Dominic?" she asked in a quiet voice. Her pulse was racing a lot faster than her calm words would indicate.

"Yes. And I just hope it's what you really want. You would not only be giving me a child, but also my parents their first grandchild. I might as well warn you that it won't be easy being the mother of the Saxon heir." Dominic's mouth set in a grim line when he added, "That might be something you need to really consider."

She knew how it was when it came to first grandchildren. Her cousin Chance's son, Marcus, had been the first for her aunt and uncle and she had been around to experience the hoopla that for years seemed endless. "I would welcome your parents' involvement in our child's life, and if they get too overbearing I believe that I'd be able to handle them."

When he didn't say anything for a while and she felt the throb in her body becoming an ache, she asked, "What is your decision, Dominic?" She stared into the intensity of his green eyes, wanting to hear him say it, refusing to assume anything.

"My decision, Taylor, is to take you to that island, spend a week with you and get you pregnant."

Taylor's breath caught in her throat. His words had been straightforward. No way for any misunderstanding. He had agreed to what she'd asked for. Confident that he could. He was giving her just what she wanted and she couldn't hide her happiness. It was there in her smile. She felt overwhelmed. Touched. Totally elated. "Thank you. It's what I want."

She didn't miss the look of desire in his eyes when he said in a deep, husky tone, "Me and you both."

Dominic knew it was time for Taylor to leave or else he would be considering things that he should not have—not at this point. Deciding to be the father of her child was enough for now.

"Did you enjoy dinner?" he asked, trying to control the situation.

"Yes."

"Good. It's getting late. I'll walk you downstairs for Ryder to take you home," he said, grabbing his jacket off the back of the sofa and slipping into it.

"I'm going home for the weekend," she said casually. He knew home to her was Charlotte, North Carolina.

"If you change your mind about anything while I'm away then—"

"I won't be changing my mind," he said in an assured tone as they walked toward the door. "In fact, I'll give my attorney a call to draw up the necessary papers." At her surprised look he said, "I'm sure you know that I'll feel better about the situation if we treat it like a legitimate business deal—which it is. That means a binding contract between us that we can agree on."

"Of course."

He glanced over at her. She said the words but to his way of thinking sounded none too pleased. Had she thought he would give her a verbal agreement on anything and not follow it up in writing? Not only would doing so protect him but it would protect her, as well. All he had to do was recall what had happened to his childhood friend Matt Caulder.

Matt had fallen in love and had gotten married a few years back. The woman had been bad news from the first, but love had blinded his friend to that fact. Within months the woman had gotten pregnant and had tried using the child as bargaining power whenever she'd wanted anything. Luckily, Matt had been able to take Rhonda to court and prove he was the better parent.

He couldn't imagine ever having to take Taylor to court for anything, but still he wanted his rights regarding any child they made together protected.

"I'll arrange for my attorney to get the papers to you within a week. That will give you time to let your own attorney review them," he said as they walked toward the bank of elevators. "Do you have any idea when we'll be leaving for the island? There're a few business matters I'd want to wrap up before then."

"In two weeks. I'm contacting my travel agent tomorrow to set everything into motion. I'm looking at the first week in April. Will that work for you?"

Whether it did or not, he intended to make it work. A week spent on an island with her was worth shifting anything around that needed to be changed. "Yes, it will work."

When they stepped onto the elevator she said, "Sorry I didn't get to meet your parents."

He nodded. He was sorry, as well. They would like her. "They were meeting friends but I thought that perhaps they would return early. I was wrong. However, considering the circumstances of our business arrangement, it's inevitable that you'll eventually meet them."

He had to continue to think of what they would be doing as a business arrangement and nothing more. He glanced over and caught her staring at him. Her head was tilted in a way that gave the impression she was trying to figure something out. Most likely it was him. Although she had been his asset manager for a couple of years she'd never really seen the personal side of him. Things had always been kept on a strictly business level.

"Will you tell your parents everything?"

"No. They have purely romantic minds and won't understand how we can do such a thing without being in love, so the less they know the better."

He sighed knowing in a few moments the elevator would be back down in the lobby. He turned to her. "Are you sure this is what you want, Taylor?"

Now he was giving her the chance to reconsider all they had agreed to this evening.

"Yes, I'm sure. I want a baby."

"In that case," he said slowly, "I'm going to try my best to give you one. To give *us* one," he clarified.

Unable to resist, he leaned forward and placed a gentle kiss on her lips. It was a lot tamer than the lip-locker, tongue-thrasher of earlier, but he still managed to feel blood sizzle through his veins. Kissing her was definitely increasing his sex drive, arousing everything male within. Considering the number of beautiful women who routinely crossed his path, he found it strange that he would want her so intensely.

The elevator door opened and he saw Ryder across the lobby, standing and talking with one of the hotel workers. The older man caught his gaze and nodded. Dominic returned his eyes to Taylor. "This is where I must bid you good-night," he said, trying to sound normal when he felt anything but. "Have a safe trip to Charlotte and I'll see you in a couple of weeks."

He tried not focusing on her lips. They were lips he wanted to kiss again and was grateful when Ryder appeared. "Make sure she gets home safely," he said.

"Sure thing."

Not able to fight temptation and not caring that

they weren't alone—besides Ryder there were a number of people mingling around in the lobby— he leaned over and kissed her lips once more. The moment he did so, tingles of awareness shot through him. The thought that suddenly jackknifed through his mind was how was he going to spend a week with her on some exotic island and maintain his control? The answer came to him just as quickly.

He wouldn't have to.

Elated beyond belief, Taylor bid the driver good-night and walked toward her front door. She glanced over her shoulder. Ryder had not moved and was still stationed by the car. Dominic had instructed the man not to leave until he saw that she was safely inside her home and Ryder was definitely following orders.

After unlocking her door she opened it and went inside. After scanning the room, she quickly moved to the windows and flipped the blinds, letting him know she was okay. It was only then that he got inside the sedan and drove off.

She checked her watch. It was almost ten. To Taylor it was still fairly early, but someone like Vanessa, who was known to retire early, would normally have been in bed by now. But Taylor knew she'd want to hear this—she had news worth sharing. She picked up the phone to begin dialing. After she talked to Vanessa she would call Cheyenne, who was doing a photo shoot somewhere in China. The three of them would be together this coming weekend in Charlotte when they got fitted for their bridesmaids' dresses.

"Hello."

Taylor raised a brow. It was a man's voice. Cameron's.

"Yes, Cameron, how are you? Is Vanessa asleep?"

She heard his smooth chuckle. "No, she's awake. Hold on a second."

Taylor really liked Cameron and, unlike Vanessa, she had from the first. It hadn't bothered her in the least that at one time he'd tried taking over her family company. She hadn't taken it personally as Vanessa had. Increasing a person's wealth was Taylor's business and she couldn't help but admire anyone who wanted to increase their riches.

"Taylor, what happened?"

Taylor rolled her eyes. "What makes you think something happened?"

"Ha! Cut the act, Taylor. We both know what was supposed to go down tonight. So give up the details!"

"Details? Why did Cameron answer your phone? Isn't it kind of late for him to be visiting?" Taylor asked, grinning.

"Nope. In fact he's staying the night. And unless I change the locks he'll stay the week. He likes keeping me in his sights and I like having him around."

Taylor could hear the smile in Vanessa's voice.

Her sister was happy and she was happy for her. In fact she was happy for herself, as well, which was the reason she had called.

"So don't change the subject. Tell me everything."

"Can we talk now or am I taking you away from something?"

"I can talk. Cameron just got in the shower," Vanessa said.

"He's agreed to do it."

"Dominic Saxon agreed to get you pregnant?"

She could hear the excitement in Vanessa's voice. "Yes."

"So I'm going to be an aunt?"

Taylor smiled. "More than likely. There's no reason to think we won't click." Especially after tonight, she thought, remembering how Dominic had to be assured that they would.

"When you come home this weekend, we're going to have to celebrate."

Biting down on her lip, Taylor fought to control her happiness and discovered that she couldn't. Both of her sisters knew how much she wanted a child.

"Can I tell Sienna?"

Taylor smiled. Sienna Bradford was Vanessa's best friend and had been since grade school. "Yes, tell her but don't tell the cousins anything. You know how overprotective they can be at times."

"Okay. So there's a chance you'll be pregnant at my wedding."

Taylor sighed. She certainly hoped so. If everything worked out as planned, she and Dominic would be going to the Caribbean the beginning of next month and Vanessa was having a June wedding. Taylor wouldn't be so far along that she needed to worry about an adjustment to her bridesmaid's dress, but she hoped to be very, merry pregnant.

"I'll let you get back to Cameron and I prefer that you not tell him. He and Morgan have a friendship," she said, thinking of her cousin, "and he might let something slip."

"I hate to say it, but you're probably right. You've taken a big step, Taylor. Are you sure you're ready for the next one?"

Taylor felt a nervous flutter in her belly, the same belly that would be her child's home for nine months. "Yes, I'm ready for the next one."

"Tell me you're joking about this, Nick."

The look on Matt Caulder's face indicated that he was expecting Dominic to say the diabolic plan he'd just laid out to him was a joke. But the more Matt studied his best friend's expression the more he could tell Dominic was dead serious.

Accepting that when Dominic made his mind up about something, then that was it, he looked back down at the brochure he'd been given before meeting Dominic's eyes again. Although he doubted it would do any good, he said, "The Caribbean is a nice place to be this time of year, but as your attorney I'm advising you not to go for what you have in mind."

Dominic had expected as much. He leaned back in his chair. He had arrived at Matt's office knowing Matt would try to talk him out of what he saw was disaster waiting to happen. Dominic saw something else waiting to happen when he arrived in the Caribbean.

"Your advice is duly noted although it won't be accepted," he said smoothly. "As my attorney, what I want is for you to draw up a document that will protect me in the event Taylor has a change of heart and doesn't want me to be a part of my child's life once she becomes pregnant."

"That can easily be done but what makes you think you're going to get her pregnant?"

Dominic smiled and stretched out his legs in front of him. "After looking at that brochure and knowing what you know about me, is there a reason I won't?"

Matt shook his head, chuckling. "No, but why this way?"

"You, the king of one-night stands, have the nerve to ask me that?"

"Mainly because I feel differently about life and love than you do."

Dominic knew that to be true. His and Matt's friendship spanned years. They seemed destined to be friends, the way he had been destined to marry Camry. Matt's mother, Deena, had been Megan's best friend in high school, and although the two had attended difference colleges, their close friendship remained intact over the years.

When Deena got pregnant from a short-term affair it was Dominic's mom she called on. Megan who had invited her to move to D.C. to stay with her until she was able to get on her feet to take on her role as a single mother. Matt was just a few months older than Dominic, but the two had been raised so close they considered each other as brothers. When Deena had died a few years ago from breast cancer it was Megan, Marcello and Dominic who had stood beside him as the only other family he had.

Dominic came to his feet. "Well, draw up something that Taylor and I can both live with and make sure it's airtight," he said, recalling what Matt had gone through with his wife, Rhonda.

"I can't wait to meet her."

Dominic shot Matt a surprised look. "Why?"

"Evidently Taylor Steele has caught your attention."

"No, her proposal has. There's nothing going on between me and Taylor other than a business arrangement."

"And you're certain that's all there is to it?"

"I want her," Dominic said honestly.

"And beyond that?"

"There's nothing beyond that."

"And again I'm going to ask if you're sure."

Dominic met Matt's unconvinced stare. "Yes, I'm absolutely and positively sure."

Chapter 4

"Welcome to the island of Latois, Mrs. Jones."

"Thank you," Taylor said as she smiled at the perky receptionist. She and Dominic had made a decision to register under a false name as a way to avoid unwanted publicity. Although the resort's management prided themselves on providing absolute privacy, the media had a way of finding out anything they wanted.

Another thing they had decided to do was to let the management and staff assume they were married. She figured most of the couples at the resort were and felt there was no reason for her and Dominic to be the oddballs.

Taylor checked her watch. She had flown in straight from D.C. and Dominic would be arriving a little later that day from New York. That would give her time to get settled and relaxed in their suite before he got there. The past two weeks had been extremely busy. After visiting with her family in Charlotte, she had attended a financial conference in Texas that had lasted an entire week.

She had spoken to Dominic only once and that was when he had called to ask if she'd found his attorney's contract satisfactory. She had. In fact her attorney had been surprised at just how fair Dominic was being. She would have full custody of the child and he would be entitled to a certain number of visits during the year. They were to rotate holidays, which she felt was reasonable. The financial package he would provide for his child was very generous; actually more than she had expected.

"An attendant will escort you to your room, Mrs. Jones."

The woman's words pulled in Taylor's thoughts. "Thank you." She took the passkey and the gift bag she was handed.

She had been given a schedule of activities for the week that included body massages for the both of them. Later that day they were to share a romantic candlelight dinner in their room.

The first thing Taylor thought when she entered her room was that the accommodations were abso-

lutely wonderful. The suite was divided into a spacious sitting area, a wet bar and a massive bedroom.
The huge windows in the bedroom provided a pano-
ramic view of the ocean. It was beautiful. Inviting.
Breathtaking. She could imagine her and Dominic
walking barefoot on the beach later in the near-
perfect spring weather.

She then took a look at the larger-than-king-size
bed that was swathed in snow-white bedcoverings
and huge fluffy pillows. It gave the room a serene
and tranquil look, totally out of sync with the hot,
passionate lovemaking that would take place
between the sheets over the next seven days. She
then thought of the lingerie she had bought, a different color and style for each and every night. Each
piece carefully chosen for its sexiness and the
ability to entice, seduce and persuade.

Taylor knew that a lot of the couples she would
meet over the next few days were fertility challenged and thought a change of climate, the removal
of stress would help the problem. She honestly
didn't think she and Dominic would have a problem
conceiving. Her main purpose in wanting to make
a baby here on the island versus back in D.C. was
wanting to conceive in style. This would be her only
child and she wanted the special moment of conception to happen in a way that would be memorable.

Something else memorable, something she couldn't
erase from her mind was the kiss she and Dominic

had shared that night in his hotel suite. She had been kissed before, many times, but nothing had sent sensations firing through her the way Dominic's lips and tongue had. She had liked it. A lot. And even now she couldn't help but anticipate it happening again. Here in this room. Plenty of times over the next week.

A visit to her doctor indicated this was her hot week, the best days to conceive, and she was more than eager to get started in making a baby. She knew it was ridiculous but she felt her body was ready, overanxious to begin. The thought of exotic foods and aphrodisiac-laden drinks were nice but she really didn't need either to want to tumble all day and night with Dominic between the sheets. She suddenly began to feel hot and on edge. Maybe the nature of this place had something to do with it.

And as she headed for the bedroom to start unpacking, she thought it was more than that. It was the anticipated arrival of one particular man.

Dominic's limo pulled in front of the Capri Resort on the private island of Latois. Just as the brochure had depicted, the place was grand, simply exquisite. Someone who was entrenched in the hotel business, as he was, could appreciate such a place from the beautifully landscaped property to the stunning ocean setting.

He checked his watch. By his calculations Taylor

should have arrived on the island hours ago. Was she in the suite waiting for him? He knew a lot of their activities for the next seven days were prearranged, but then a lot of them weren't. One thing the resort encouraged was couples spending a lot of private time together, preferably in their suite in bed procreating. He definitely didn't have a problem with that. In fact he was looking forward to it.

A few minutes later upon checking in, he was told his wife had arrived and was in their suite. He was given his own passkey and a bottle of their house champagne, which, he'd been informed, contained a special potent ingredient intended to boost their sexual drive. The clerk hadn't batted an eye when she'd said it.

After stepping onto the elevator that would take him up to the tenth floor, in no time at all it seemed, he had reached his floor and was walking down the long hallway toward his room. The bellman would be bringing up his bags later.

When he stood in front of the suite's door he swallowed hard, knowing what the week entailed. He had tried not to notice the couples he'd passed and just how openly amorous they were with each other. Another thing he noticed was that unlike a lot of resorts, there weren't a lot of people out and about. Most were probably busy behind closed doors trying to accomplish what they had come here to do.

He opened the door and stepped inside the exact moment Taylor was walking out of the bedroom area. Immediately their gazes locked. He was rendered momentarily speechless by how quickly blood shot from his head straight to his groin. His mouth suddenly felt dry and every muscle in his body—some more so than others—felt hard as a rock.

She was wearing a light blue sundress with spaghetti straps that revealed just what beautiful shoulders she had. An ample amount of cleavage was showing, enough to make him appreciate the firm shape of her breasts, as well. Then there was her face and well-defined features. He decided at that moment that Taylor wasn't just beautiful; she was what fantasies were made of. There was an inborn sensuality about her that had been hidden behind her business suits. The business suits represented her profession. The outfit she had on now showed her perfection, especially her curvy figure.

"Dominic."

His name was spoken in a soft tone and he watched her hands come to rest at her sides. For some reason he'd always enjoyed looking at her hands whenever she met with him and flipped through papers she would have for him to sign. Her nails were always neat with a French manicure displaying a nonflashy look. The same extended to her fingers. Some women liked showing off their diamonds practically on every finger. But Taylor didn't even wear a ring, Her hands were long and graceful. Elegant. Sturdy. And he could just imagine those hands touching him, caressing the length of his hardened…

He sucked in a deep breath when he saw where his thoughts were headed. He closed the door behind him as he tried to maintain his control, but found himself losing it and quickly recalled how long it had been since he'd had a woman for a bed partner and decided it had been way too long.

"Aren't we on speaking terms?" she said as a teasing smile touched her lips.

Instead of answering her, he placed the bottle of champagne on a nearby table and crossed the room to her. There was no need for formality. They both knew why they were there and as far as he was concerned, now was just as good a time as any to get the ball rolling. And speaking of balls…he felt his thicken. His testosterone level was so high that he wouldn't be surprised if he were to impregnate her with twins.

The thought of such a thing actually happening made him that much more aroused. It actually made his body ache. Seeing her again was doing a job on him, a real exclusive number. He couldn't recall ever wanting a woman so badly. When he stood directly in front of her, he reached out and cupped the back of her neck to guide her mouth to meet his.

The moment their lips touched he felt it. Passion

so thick you could lap it up. Spread it about. Get smothered by it. And when he went past her moist lips and inserted his tongue inside her mouth, he knew he had been anticipating this very moment ever since the night they had dined together over two weeks ago.

Her response was immediate, absolute and totally delectable. The reason they were here might be staged, predestined so to speak, but the sexual chemistry between them was as instant and spontaneous as it could get. The depth of her sensuality was enough to make him want to jump in the ocean to cool off. A cold shower just wouldn't work off the heat. He had discovered over the past two weeks, ever since she had placed her proposal into his lap and he had accepted, that he desired her to the point of madness. And this was the result. He was getting a pretty good taste of her and she was getting a good taste of him, as well.

He heard her groan low in her throat and knew if he pushed hard enough they would be making love right here, possibly on the floor, which wasn't where he wanted his son or daughter conceived. He knew she could feel how aroused he was from the way his body was pressed against hers. He wanted her to feel it. Get used to it.

He really did need to slow down, he thought, as he continued to lap her up. He would take things slow the next time around. But now this seemed appropriate. This is what he wanted. And he was struck by the enormity of just how much passion was in one single kiss. Of how much tongue action was required. He was enjoying sharing both with her. There was nothing gentle about the kiss. Far from it. There was hunger, greed and a desperation he hadn't been used to before, but was getting familiar with now. For some reason she felt right in his arms. Right in his mouth. Right with her body pressed intimately against his.

It wasn't easy, but he finally gained control and pulled back. She gasped for breath the moment their mouths separated. After pulling air into his own lungs he leaned back close to her, lowered his head close to her ear and whispered in a deep, husky tone, "Hmm, so much for us not being on speaking terms."

For a full minute Taylor was speechless, too awed to form any kind of coherent words. It was hard to believe that this was the man with whom, until three weeks ago, she'd shared a strictly professional relationship. And now what they were about to share was anything but that. And considering the reason they were there, she could hardly suggest to him to slow down.

Her heart was racing as she stood rooted in place. Dominic, however, seemed rather at ease, unerringly calm, as he walked over to the sofa to remove his jacket.

"I take it you had a nice flight here?"

She blinked upon realizing he had spoken. She glanced across the room at him and felt a sweet craving invade her body. The man was simply gorgeous and exuded a degree of sensuality that should be outlawed. He was wearing an expensive tailored shirt with a pair of dark slacks. He was tall and lean. His shoulders were broad and his hips narrow. What a body! She didn't want to think about that same body, naked and in bed with her, flesh to flesh.

"Taylor?"

It was then she realized she hadn't answered his question. She pulled in a rather shaky sigh. "Yes, it was nice. What about yours?"

He stood beside the sofa. His hair was loose and flowing around his shoulders and his feet were braced apart, again making her conscious of what a good-looking man he was and what a fine physique he had. He was in great shape and she would undoubtedly find out just how great later that night.

"The same. I took a nap so now I'm pretty well rested."

Taylor swallowed. Was he giving her fair warning? His expression was inscrutable and she couldn't tell by his eyes what he was thinking.

"What's this?" he asked, picking up the gift bag off the sofa.

She looked at the bag he had in his hand. "That's

something I was given at check-in. I haven't had a chance to see what's in it."

"We may as well take a look together," he said. The first thing he pulled out was a book. His chuckle made her wonder what type of book it was. He glanced over at her, evidently saw her curious expression and said, "I guess you can call it a self-help manual. It's titled *Best Sexual Positions for Baby-Making*." He flipped through the pages and looked back up at her. "There are even pictures. Umm, interesting."

She could just imagine, but even if curiosity killed her, she would not cross the room to take a peep. He placed the book on the table next to the sofa as though he intended to take time to delve between the pages more later. He then pulled out several jars of what looked like creams and other items. He proved her right when he said, "An assortment of flavored creams, a bottle of lickable lotion and several gels. This feminine arousal gel I would assume is for you and the erection gel is for me."

Taylor's gaze automatically shifted to his crotch. She was staring at it, but at the moment she couldn't help herself, imagining…

"There's also a notice about a free movie they're showing tonight on the television. It's guaranteed to put us in the mood if we're not already there," he was saying.

The thought that crossed Taylor's mind at that exact

moment was that literally, she couldn't speak for him but she was already there. In fact her body didn't rightly seem connected to her brain. It wanted to do one thing while her brain was trying to drill some sense into her. She really wasn't paying attention.

"There's also a notice that dinner will be served in our room around six." He checked his watch. "That's a couple of hours away. Is there anything you'd like to do until then?"

Taylor took a deep breath while thinking that, yes, there was something she would like to do until then. Jumping his bones seemed like an activity worth trying. But she knew she couldn't do that. She had put too much work into her seduction scene tonight to get carried away by a few errant hormones. Well, maybe more than a few.

"What about a walk on the beach?" she decided to ask.

From the look on his face she could tell her suggestion surprised him. "A walk on the beach?"

"Yes, and then we can return to the room and shower for dinner," she said.

"Ok, then let's take a walk on the beach."

She glanced at his clothes. Not the typical attire for walking on the beach. "Do you want to change first?"

He smiled. "No, I'm fine."

He most certainly was.

He moved toward the door. Paused and glanced over his shoulder. "Are you coming?"

Not yet, she thought, but she had a feeling that's all she would be doing later tonight underneath his hard, muscular body. "Yes," she said, crossing the room to where he was standing. He smiled again and she felt all kinds of flutters fill her stomach. She couldn't wait until tonight.

Dominic thought the same thing as he walked beside Taylor on the long stretch of beach. He couldn't remember ever taking the time to do something so relaxing. He definitely hadn't ever done so with Camry. Their lives had been fast paced—jet-setters—with no thought of settling down and taking things slow or making a family. They'd figured that would come later. And they had been so wrong.

Not wanting to think of his life with Camry—and what he'd lost with her death—he wanted to concentrate on what he would gain with Taylor. Since he had no intentions of every marrying again, at least he would have a son or daughter who would inherit what he was working so hard to acquire. His own Saxon dynasty.

He had removed his shoes and socks and actually liked the feel of the sand beneath his feet. He also liked having this woman beside him. They continued walking down the long stretch of beach. The sugar-white sand gave way to a clear blue-green sea and the scent of the ocean filled his nostrils. Taylor wasn't saying much but then neither was he. He was too busy thinking of what he would love to be doing with all those jars of flavored creams this week. What he *intended* to do with them.

"The beach is simply gorgeous, isn't it?"

He turned his head and caught her gaze. His eyes moved to her lips, remembering how they'd tasted and a sensation passed through his body. "Yes, it is," he responded, thinking so was she. "I can't recall the last time I've done something like this."

"Really?" she said, looking at him. "But you own an entire island on the ocean."

He wasn't surprised she knew that. Other than his parents, Matt and the IRS, she was the only other person who knew the vast extent of his wealth. The media thought they knew but in essence they really didn't have a clue. His grandfather was determined to make sure Dominic took his place as the rightful Saxon heir and had set up various accounts for him in all parts of the world. Dominic wanted no part of it and to this day refused to acknowledge the old man's generosity. Dominic was determined not to accept his grandfather's money, which he saw as a device Franco Saxon was using to alleviate his guilt and buy his way into his grandson's affections. As far as Dominic was concerned, it would not happen.

"Yes, I own that island but I rarely have time to enjoy it. You of all people should know how busy I am."

It seemed he was driven to accumulate even more

wealth and was beginning to believe the accusa-
tions his father had once made were true. As long
as he maintained a degree of his own wealth, he
would not be tempted to accept what his grandfather was offering.

"In that case I'm glad at least you have this week
to relax and unwind."

He chuckled. "Um, is that what I'll be doing?"

Her grin was almost contagious when she said,
"Somewhat. But I promise it will be a week you'll
remember."

She sounded confident. Certain. But then he was
also convinced it would be a week he would remember. Deciding he needed to talk about something,
anything that would take his mind off bedding her,
he said, "I understand your sister is getting married
in June to Cameron Cody."

She glanced at him. "Yes. You know Cameron?"

"Yes. We've met. We've even been partners in a
few business ventures. He's an astute businessman."

"So are you. It doesn't surprise me that you know
Cameron. We met when he tried to take over my
family's business."

Dominic lifted a brow. "You're kidding, right?"

She smiled. "No, I'm not kidding. It was supposed to be a hostile takeover, but he never got all
the voting shares he needed."

"So your family became friends with him instead?" he asked, amazed. He'd been involved in a

few takeover attempts himself. The last thing the parties involved felt toward each other afterward, regardless of whether the attempt had been successful or not, was friendliness.

"Yes, at least, my four male cousins did," she was saying. "It was a male thing. I think they admired Cameron's tenacity and respected his drive to succeed. They never saw him as a threat because the Steele family is so close, so we weren't worried about anyone defecting. But Cameron had to learn a valuable lesson."

"Which was?"

"No matter what, blood is thicker than money. And trust me, he was offering a lot. But for us it wasn't about the money. It was about the legacy that my father and uncle passed on to us. They started the company many years ago and had always intended for it to be family owned and operated."

Dominic nodded. "And now Cameron will become a part of your family."

"Yes, he will be. He loves my sister very much and she loves him."

Love. He was familiar with that word because of his parents but had yet to experience the emotion himself. He had loved Camry but not in the same way that he knew his father loved his mother. What he'd felt for his wife had been more fondness than love. They respected each other and were good friends during their brief marriage.

"Ready to head back?"

Taylor had stopped walking and was smiling politely at him. "Yes, I can certainly use that shower," he said.

And he could also use something else. Something he was looking forward to getting later.

"Are you going to take a shower with me?"

Dominic's question made Taylor's stomach lurch in heated lust. An ache started at the juncture of her legs. They had returned from their walk on the beach and were standing in the bedroom. He had wasted no time removing his shirt and stood with his hands in his pockets, which caused the material of his pants to stretch tight against his thighs. And they were such muscular thighs.

She cleared her throat to swallow the lump that had formed there. "I'd rather wait until later, after we make love."

He looked amused at her statement. "And may I ask why?"

Yes, *why?* She shrugged. "Although we won't know the exact moment it happens, I know that I will get pregnant from you this week and I'd rather not let the first time we come together be in a shower."

He gave her a smile that intensified that ache in her body. "You don't think we can share a shower without making love?"

"What do you think?" she countered.

He stared at her for a moment, in that way that always got to her, making her hot all over, as his gaze traveled up and down her body. Finally, he said, "I think that you're probably right."

Oh, yeah, I am right, trust me, she thought. "I'll wait in the other room for you to finish and then I'll take my shower," she said, heading for the door.

"Taylor?"

She turned back around. "Yes?"

"I think you should know that I want you."

She saw the heat in his eyes, felt the lust and desire in them from across the room. She was no novice at being wanted by a man, but this was the first time she could actually feel the intensity. And what was so amazing was that she craved him just as much.

"Thanks for telling me," she said softly. "And I want you, too." She decided to lay her cards on the table since he was laying down his.

"Come here. I want to give you something to think about while I'm in the shower alone," was his comeback in a husky tone.

She started to tell him that it wasn't necessary. She had enough to think about already. But she figured he was going to kiss her again, which she didn't have any qualms with. She was looking forward to it. Her lips were still tingling from their last encounter.

She retraced her steps and crossed the room to him, trying not to focus on his naked chest and finding it hard not to do so. Especially downward, where the sprinkle of hair seemed to take a low path toward his waist, even lower toward his...

"Taylor?"

She shifted her gaze from his chest to his eyes. "Yes?" She'd been caught staring.

He didn't say anything for a moment; he just continued to look at her, especially her mouth. And the more he stared the more her lips itched for him to taste them. "I'm going to enjoy being here with you for the next seven days," he said, as he reached out and untied the straps at her shoulders, and then gave each a quick tug.

She hadn't been expecting it and before she could blink, the top of her sundress dropped and she was naked to the waist. She opened her mouth to say something and that's when he inserted his tongue inside. At that moment she forgot about everything else except what his mouth was doing to hers. He was part French and she wondered if it was an inborn part of a Frenchman's nature to master the art of French-kissing, because he certainly had. She would even go so far as to say he was an expert. She'd been French-kissed before but never like this. His tongue was definitely a weapon of mass seduction.

Automatically, she angled her head to get more of the pleasure. If this was what he wanted to give her to think about then he was succeeding. He had her thinking. He also had her panties getting wet.

He released her mouth. They were standing so close, their lips mere inches apart, as if ready to go at it again, devour each other senseless, when she discovered the kiss wasn't all he wanted to give her to think about. She sucked in a deep breath when she felt his fingers touch her breasts. At that moment her brain seemed to turn to mush. He cupped her breasts in his hands and began ardently caressing them, letting the tips of his fingers rub gently across her hardened nipples.

He met her gaze and the heat she saw in the depths of his green eyes made her a lost cause. At that moment she wanted to make love to him and she didn't care if they conceived their child right there, while standing up. She wondered if that particular position was in that little book.

He lowered his mouth to her breasts and like a vacuum he sucked a hardened tip into his mouth. Then his tongue went to work like a man famished for the taste of her. She responded with a soft moan and reached out and sank her fingers in his hair to hold his head to her, experiencing a heated breakdown of all her senses. Her stomach began quivering with a need that was as intense as anything she'd ever encountered.

She let out a deep, startled moan when he suddenly slipped a warm hand under her dress and immediately went to the area between her legs. Slipping underneath her panties, he planted his fingers in her sensitive flesh. Blood pounded in her ears when he began stroking her intimately. She wasn't sure what was sending her over the edge the fastest, his mouth or his fingers. She released a soft sigh when he intensified the kiss at the same time he increased the tempo of the stroke of his fingers.

He was showing no mercy. She tightened her grip on his head and called out his name when a shudder of immense proportions rammed through her, shaking her to the core. She squeezed her eyes shut when everything in the room seemed to come rushing together, bearing down on them. She could barely stand and her mind was void of any conscious thought except the intense pleasure ripping through her.

When he finally released her it took a few moments to get her mind back in check. She opened her eyes and nearly lost it again when he took his finger, the same one that had intimately stroked her, and brought it to his lips and tasted it.

The corners of his mouth distended into a serious smile when he said in a huskily erotic voice. "Take my word for it. The last thing you need tonight is arousing gel."

Chapter 5

At the sound of the shower going Taylor expelled a sigh. She then began pacing the room, needing to do something. Otherwise, she would be tempted to strip off her clothes and join Dominic.

The man had given her one hell of an orgasm just from foreplay. She didn't want to think just how explosive the real thing would be. If his aim had been to prep her for tonight then he had succeeded—she was set on go. In fact, she'd been ready for Dominic ever since he had agreed to this week.

The ache returned to her body just picturing him standing naked in the shower under a spray of water. She'd gotten a glimpse of his chest, more than a glimpse actually. Before she had left the bedroom, he had pulled her in his arms, letting her taste the essence of herself off his lips. Her naked breasts had pressed against his bare chest, and the contact had nearly given her another orgasm. She had a history of being someone not prone to climax easily. In fact, usually it would take a while for any man to light her fire to the degree where she would want to make love more than once in one night.

Deciding she needed to sit down and relax she dropped down on the sofa and then out of curiosity, she picked up the book Dominic had pulled out of the gift bag earlier. Her eyes widened at each page. She hadn't known there were so many positions a couple could use. Not surprisingly, it said the best position to conceive was man on top. It didn't take much to fantasize about Dominic on top of her in bed, inside her body and...

She stood up and tossed the book on the table, deciding she'd imagined enough for now. She needed to take her mind off things, namely sex and Dominic. After he finished his shower, she would take hers, and then they would get ready for dinner, which would be delivered to their room at exactly six o'clock. Once dinner arrived their night of initiating conception would begin. Lord, she hoped they made it through dinner because they would need all their strength for later.

One way to get her mind off Dominic, she decided, would be to call Vanessa and talk to her for a short minute. She had spent time with her sisters while home getting fitted for the bridesmaids' dresses. It didn't go unnoticed by her that Cheyenne wasn't as talkative as she usually was and looked a little on the thin side. Not that her sister's perfect model figure still didn't look to die for. Vanessa had picked up on it, too, and had pulled her to the side and asked her if she knew what was wrong with their baby sister. She didn't have a clue then and didn't have one now. As far as they knew it couldn't be man trouble since Cheyenne didn't have a steady beau.

Crossing the room, Taylor pulled her mobile phone from her purse and clicked on Vanessa's number. She smiled when Cameron answered. That, she noticed, was becoming a norm. "Hi, Cameron, is Vanessa around?"

"Yes. Hold on."

Moments later her sister came on the line. "Taylor, are you okay?"

Taylor lifted a brow. Vanessa sounded breathless, like someone who had run a marathon. Or someone who had just finished making love.

"Yes, I'm okay. Sounds like you're okay, as well," she couldn't help but say. She knew if she was there she would see a huge blush on her sister's face.

Vanessa gave a shaky laugh and said, "Well, yeah, I'm okay. Cameron is here."

"So I notice. Am I interrupting anything?"

There was a pause and then. "No, I'm fine. Cameron just went into the kitchen. He's going to do the cooking tonight. I was hoping you would call. How are things going?"

"Fine. I arrived here around eleven o'clock today and Dominic got here around two. We've taken a walk on the beach."

"That's all?"

She shook her head. Her sister had turned into a regular little miss hot pants since hooking up with Cameron. Vanessa figured just because she spent most of her free time in bed that everyone else should do the same. "Yes, that's all. We don't want to rush anything. We have all week."

"Nothing like getting a head start. The more you do it, the better your chances of getting pregnant, right?"

"Right, but it only takes one good time and according to the doctor I'm all set. I took my temperature early and now's the time. He said it's important for me to make love a day or two before I ovulate and then the day of."

"That sounds so technical. Just roll with the flow."

Taylor smiled. "Have you heard from Cheyenne?"

"No. Have you?"

"No."

"Really, Taylor, I'm worried about her. She looked somewhat under the weather when she was here a few weeks ago. I called last night but got her machine. I told her to call me back but so far she hasn't."

"Is she out on a photo shoot?"

"No. She talked to Mom last week and told her she had come down with the flu. She was canceling her trip to Ethiopia and remaining at her Jamaican home to get some rest. She probably hasn't been eating right and her resistance is down. I'm going to try calling her again tonight. I'm really going to give her a good looking-over when she flies in for Marcus's graduation in a few weeks."

Taylor nodded. Their cousin Marcus, Chance's oldest son, would be graduating from high school. The family was excited about his acceptance into Yale University. "Okay. Let me know if you get Cheyenne and she tells you anything. Like you, I think she hasn't been eating properly."

"Do you plan on leaving your phone turned on during the time you're on that island?"

"No, but I will make it a point to check my messages."

Vanessa laughed. "Do you think Dominic is going to give you the time to do that?"

She knew what Vanessa was insinuating. "I'm going to take the time regardless."

"If Dominic Saxon is the man I think he is, the man I read about in all those magazines, you won't have time to do much all week but stay on your back."

"Vanessa!"

"Just being honest, so get prepared."

At that moment Taylor heard a sound behind her and turned around. Dominic was standing in the doorway that separated the sitting room from the bedroom, still wet from his shower with only a towel wrapped around his waist. The heat in his eyes, the ones staring at her, were scorching. She swallowed the lump in her throat.

"Vanessa, I've got to go." Taylor clicked off the phone without waiting for her sister's response. She was suddenly filled with the thought that even if she tried, there was no way to get prepared for Dominic.

"The shower is yours, Taylor. But let me go on record as saying this is the last time I plan on taking a shower alone while we're here."

Dominic didn't even attempt to understand why he was so adamant about that. Probably because all the time he had spent in the shower, standing under the jets of the water, he'd been thinking of how it would be to have Taylor in there with him, all the things they could do. *Would* do.

"And if I protest?" she asked with a teasing smile on her face.

Of course, she could protest, but he figured she wouldn't. He would make sure of it. Besides, any woman who got as hot as she did just from a man kissing her, stroking her intimately, wouldn't be hard to persuade. Not only had he felt her heat, he had tasted it. "Go ahead, if you think that you can."

The look that suddenly appeared in her eyes let him know he had been right—she would be wasting time to try to deny him. They clicked. They would probably burn up the sheets. And in the end, they would make a baby. For some reason he felt very confident about that.

His gaze roamed up and down her. She had fixed what he'd done to her sundress, but he much preferred seeing it down to her waist. He liked her breasts. The feel of them in his hand. The taste of them in his mouth.

He saw she hadn't moved from the spot. "Aren't you going to take your shower now...or do you prefer we get into something else?"

She crossed her arms over her breasts. "You're blocking the doorway."

"Oh. You don't think I'd let you get by?"

She chuckled. "Not without trying something."

He smiled. "I thought one of the perks for this week is for me to try just about anything."

"Yes, but the key is perfect timing."

His smile widened. "Trust me, every time we come together will be perfect" He stepped away from the doorway. "Go ahead. I'll behave."

She gave him an *I don't believe you* look, before heading toward the bathroom. When she got close by him she slowed her steps and looked at him up and down. "Something wrong?" he asked.

"No, nothing's wrong."

"Then I can only assume that you like what you see, Taylor Steele."

She met his gaze and his heart began thudding hard with the look in her eyes. "Yeah, I like what I see."

"Do you want it?" he asked, feeling a sizzle low in his belly.

She tilted her head at an angle that got his attention because it made him see just what a beautiful neckline she had. "Not only do I want it, Dominic, I plan on getting plenty of it. Later."

When she slipped by him and went into the bedroom and closed the door, a heated rush flooded his insides at her bold statement. As far as he was concerned, later couldn't get here quick enough to suit him.

Taylor leaned back against the door the moment she shut it behind her and breathed in a deep, shaky breath. How on earth was she supposed to get through dinner when Dominic exuded so much temptation? And he knew exactly what he was doing to her. She didn't have to be convinced that he was a man who knew how to please a woman in bed. There was no doubt in her mind that he would please her. And just thinking about the degree of pleasure she would receive made her weak in the knees.

When she thought her wobbly legs could support her, she moved away from the door toward the drawers where she had placed her undergarments earlier after she'd unpacked. She would get everything she needed now before coming out of the bathroom after her shower. Chances were Dominic would use the room to dress for dinner and she wasn't ready to walk in on him while she was half-naked. Grabbing a bra and a pair of panties out of the drawer, she headed for the bathroom, taking time to grab one of the courtesy bathrobes out of the closet.

After a walk on the beach she needed the shower, but more than anything, she needed to take a shower to cool off.

Except for the sound of the shower, the suite seemed quiet, Dominic thought as he finished dressing. Never before had he wanted a woman the way he wanted Taylor. He was beginning to feel restless, on edge, horny. He couldn't help thinking of just how sexy she was, and how much she seemed to enjoy his kisses. He took pleasure in the art of seduction and kissing was just one of the elements he used. There were numerous others and he planned to put each one into practice before leaving the island.

It didn't take much to see that Taylor was a very passionate woman and she wasn't trying to be coy about it. He could tell she was someone who was

confident with the degree of her own sensuality.
But not to the point where it swelled her head. And
she had to be one of the most positive people he
knew. He had discovered that fact the first time they
had met. She wasn't all somber and serious like
most financial advisors tended to be. He recalled her
saying once that she believed that one of the biggest
secrets to achieving what you wanted in life was
believing that you could. Just the way she believed
that the two of them would make a baby this week.
And because she believed it, he was convinced, as
well.

There was no doubt in his mind that she would
be a good mother. In his opinion his mother had
been a stellar mom, and, although Taylor was fairly
young, she possessed his mom's strong characteristics, as well. It amazed him at times how she had
the ability to feel him out before he could utter a
single word. And he liked the way she always kept
her cool. She wasn't one to freak out or get frazzled
easily—like the time he had invested a large sum of
money without consulting her and had come close
to losing it all.

Then there was her playful side. Once when she
had detected him getting tense about a risky business venture, she had encouraged him to take time
off and go with her to Coney Island for an afternoon
of fun. Officially that had been their first date,
although at the time he hadn't thought of it as such.

But still, she had shown him how important it was to occasionally get in touch with your carefree side, something he failed to do often enough.

Deciding that since he had finished dressing there was no reason to linger around in the bedroom, he walked into the sitting room. For his peace of mind he felt the best thing to do was to remove himself from temptation's way. Put his mind on something else. So he thought about his parents. He had spoken to them yesterday. After spending two weeks in France they were back in the U.S. According to them, Franco Saxon's health had greatly improved. Conversely, they had known that Dominic really didn't give a royal damn but his mother had mentioned it anyway. There had been so many times when he'd been younger, when after hearing his classmates talk about their grandparents and what a blessing they were in their lives, that he had longed for grandparents of his own. His father had told him his mother—Dominic's grandmother— had died when he was a little boy, but his grandfather was in France. As a young boy, Dominic could not understand if he had a grandfather that existed, why he never came to visit to spend time with him like his friends' grandparents had.

Much to his parents' credit, they had never spoken ill of Franco Saxon. Over the years they had accepted the older man's decision not to be a part of their lives. It was only when Dominic was

grown that he discovered why his grandfather was
not a part of his life. And it was a reason Dominic
had found unacceptable.

His ears suddenly perked up. The shower was no
longer going, which meant Taylor was finished with
that particular segment of her toiletry. Dominic
could imagine her damp body wrapped in one of
those huge fluffy towels. He wished he was there
to dry her off and thought of just how he would
complete the task. He would go slow, taking time
to pamper every inch of her body, starting with
those luscious breasts he had tasted earlier, then
moving lower to her flat stomach and small waist
and then to that gorgeous pair of legs.

He sighed deeply. It was self-torture just thinking
about all the things he would do after that. There
was no denying that he wanted Taylor and he'd told
her as much. But she wasn't fully aware of the intensity of that want. It had literally turned into a deep,
throbbing need. A need that wouldn't go away.

Taylor looked at the outfit she had chosen to wear
to dinner tonight, a black clingy halter dress. But
nothing, she thought, would raise Dominic's temperature quicker than the sexy red lace, sheer mesh
baby-doll nightie with a matching G-string that she
would put on later. It was seductive. It was daring.

Why wait till later?

She licked her lips at the thought of the sweet

torment Dominic would endure if she appeared at dinner wearing it. No doubt she would become the main entrée. She liked the thought of that.

Taylor stared at the outfit that hung in the closet a few seconds longer before deciding what she would do. Crossing the room, she pulled the red piece of lingerie out of the drawer and tossed it on the bed. It was time to turn the heat up a notch.

Dominic straightened in the chair, feeling his body get hard. The last thing he should be doing was sitting here looking through a book showing various sexual positions while waiting for Taylor. But he couldn't help himself. The pictures were definitely sexually arousing. There was not one position he couldn't picture him and Taylor trying. And if he played his cards right, before the week was out, they would try every one of them.

A faint smile touched his lips. He could just imagine the joy he would see on his parents' faces the day he told them they would be expecting a grandchild. There was no doubt in his mind that they would make wonderful grandparents. Taylor would have to be resigned to the fact that his parents would set out to make sure their grandchild was thoroughly spoiled.

"Dominic."

He turned his head to the whispered sound of his name. *Holy hell!* he thought, coming to his feet.

His mouth dropped. Blood rushed through his

veins, his heart was pounding in his chest and his pulse was beating erratically. His already hot body suddenly burst into flames. Desire. Intense chemistry. Sexual need. All three hung in the air like a sensuous mist and seeped through the material of his shirt to tantalize his skin and shoot his testosterone level through the roof.

And when she moved away from the door, slowly crossing the room toward him, his mouth was suddenly dry and his body flared into an erection he couldn't hide even if he wanted to. He could only stare and come to grips with the enormity of his desire for her. She had to be wearing one of the sexiest scraps of lingerie he'd ever seen on a woman. And if Taylor thought she could sit at a table across from him wearing something like that, she definitely had another think coming.

She came to a stop in front of him and he stared into her eyes, fully understanding the message in her gaze. "Would you be terribly upset if I asked that we postpone dinner for a while?" she asked in a deep, sultry tone.

He gave her what had to be a heated smile before taking a step closer to her with his total concentration on her mouth. "Only on one condition."

"And what condition is that?"

He was still looking at her mouth. Inched his lips down closer to it. "That you let me devour *you* instead."

He watched her lips form into a sultry smile. "Only on one condition," she countered.

Now it was his turn to ask, "And what condition is that?"

She moved her lips closer to his and murmured in a soft, sexy tone, "That I get to devour you, as well."

His body immediately responded to her words, but before he could fully react, she wrapped her hands around his neck and connected their mouths. When his lips parted on a low groan, she took full advantage of the opening and darted her tongue inside. Consumed by desire so intense that it shook him to the core, he began mating his tongue with hers in a French kiss intended to rattle her the same way she was rattling him, and destined to build a need within her to the degree he was experiencing.

Their kiss was hot. It was passionate. It was possessive. At that moment they claimed the right to belong to each other for the next seven days. To fulfill each other's fantasies, give in to each other's desires. And most important, to create a life. Tongues mingled hotly, explored greedily and devoured incessantly.

He broke off the kiss just long enough to sweep her into his arms. "We're about to burn up the sheets, Taylor," he said on a low growl, and he began walking toward the bedroom. And that, he thought, would just be the beginning.

* * *

Taylor gazed up at Dominic, drawn to the intensity of his green eyes. They were eyes that underscored what he'd said earlier. They would burn up the sheets. He wanted her. She wanted him. She was his for the taking. He was hers. Simply stated, they were two passionate individuals who were answering the mating call in the most primitive way.

When he laid her down on the bed, their gazes locked and she felt the heat of his desire all the way to her toes. It was affecting her the most at the center of her legs, an ache that was about to get satisfied.

She watched as he took a step back away from the bed and leaned over and began removing his shoes and socks. Straightening, he took off his shirt to expose his muscular chest. Tossing it aside, he then went for the zipper of his trousers. Her breath held as he slowly eased it down and while doing so he kept his gaze fastened on hers.

When he lowered his pants, along with his briefs, to the floor, her gaze shifted and went directly to his midsection, then lower. There it lingered while taking in the glory of his manhood, the enormity of his erection that accentuated the degree of his arousal. He was big, thick and hard. And there was no doubt in her mind to the degree of his need.

Or hers.

She wanted to reach out and touch him, hold his hard, warm flesh in her hands. Slide her fingers all over it and feel its texture, its strength and its heat. Her gaze shifted to his face. As if he had read her thoughts, he gave her a slow smile before moving his completely naked body toward the bed.

Taylor inhaled a deep breath and whispered his name the moment he placed one knee on the bed and reached for her. She rose up and went into his arms willingly, without haste, and the moment he leaned over and captured her mouth, she knew she was a goner. His mouth was hotter than before. It ignited every cell in her body, causing low groans to circulate in her throat, get caught in her lungs.

Then his mouth became demanding, excruciatingly dominant in a way that made her stomach clench. And when he suddenly pulled back, she inhaled deeply before lifting her gaze to his.

He didn't say anything. He simply reached out and with a flick of his wrist, in one smooth move he took off her gown and tossed it aside.

"Red is my favorite color and I liked it." He murmured the words against her throat, seconds before she felt the gentle nip of his teeth, the lap of his tongue and the sucking on the soft skin of her neck. She knew what he had just done. He had put a passion mark there, branding her as his. If there ever was a man designed to make her a mother by giving her a baby, he was.

"You're beautiful."

His words, spoken as a deep growl from his

throat, had her lifting her face up to his. The heated desire in the gaze looking back at her made her heart beat that much faster in her chest. And when he reached out and trailed his fingers from the top of her shoulders down to the twin peaks of her breasts, she swallowed deeply, trying not to detonate from his touch alone. His touch was smooth and slow, as if he would not be rushed, and when he reached her nipples, he took his fingertips and gently caressed each hardened bud with a skill and a purpose that shot intense hunger through her. Then he leaned down and his tongue outlined each tip, before taking them in his mouth one at a time and gently sucking on them the way their child would. And with each tug she felt the intensity of her need for him in the center of her legs.

"Dominic!"

He reached down and his hands found their mark between her legs. She was hot, wet and ready. And there was that annoying ache that she needed him to take away. Intense emotions were tearing into her and creating a raw need she had never felt before.

"And now I give you my baby," he rasped near her ear.

Dominic's words, both confident and arrogant, nearly took her breath away. But she didn't have time to think about that when she suddenly found herself flat on her back beneath him. His masculine physique towered over her, every perfectly formed muscle.

She looked up into his eyes, locked in his gaze the moment he gripped her hips and raised them to him. Then he entered her. It was a joining so grand, so absolute that it almost brought tears to her eyes. Her body automatically gave in to him, stretched for him. And when he began moving, it had her trembling inside. Heat flared within her, taking over her mind and body with an intensity that shook her to the core. But Dominic didn't let up. He painstakingly increased the tempo, amplified the pace. Holding her body immobile beneath his, he began pumping into her nonstop with possessive deliberation, timeless precision.

Taylor's body was suddenly hit with something akin to an electrical shock and she felt her muscles clenching, tightening. She pulled him deeper inside of her when waves of pleasure consumed her body. The exact moment she came, he did, as well, and she heard Dominic's deep, guttural growl and felt his hot release shoot to her womb.

He bucked inside her again at the same time she felt the warmth of his breath on her lips mere seconds before he took her mouth with a hunger that sent her over the edge yet again. Sensations rippled through her body when she was hurled into yet another orgasm and felt intense pleasure consume every part of her.

Dominic had been right. They were burning up the sheets.

Chapter 6

Dominic felt himself floating back down to earth after having soared to the stars and beyond. He felt as if he'd had an out-of-body experience and had been blasted right out of this hemisphere. There had never been a time when he'd made love to a woman and had been left feeling that way. He lay there transfixed, drained and completely satisfied.

But still, that didn't keep him from wondering what the hell had happened. Why even now, when Taylor was trying hard to catch her own breath, he wanted to make love to her again, detonate into another explosion. How had it come to this?

Maybe it had been that sexy red much-of-nothing

nightie she'd been wearing. Or it could have been the fact that the last time he'd made love to a woman had been months ago. And just possibly, it could have been that damn book he'd been flipping through earlier, seeing all those different lovemaking positions in vivid color. He knew any number of things could have raised his testosterone to a degree that even after two orgasms still had him hard and refusing to disconnect his body from hers. That was the strangest thing of all. Never had he made love to a woman and not wanted to come out of her afterward. But with Taylor, he liked the thought they were still intimately joined.

"You haven't gone down."

He moved to let his gaze rest on her eyes. An incredulous look glazed their depths with that observation. "No, I haven't," he admitted, feeling his erection harden even more as he spoke. "I like being inside you." And that wasn't a lie, not even close to a mild exaggeration.

He then ran his eyes over the rest of her. She was lying on her side facing him, her naked skin a dark hue against the sharp whiteness of the bedspread. Her breasts were full and firm, her stomach taut and flat with a small tattoo of a panther near her hip bone. That was the most of what he saw, since his leg was thrown over her, locking her body in place to his. He had her in one hell of a pose.

Even now what was so vividly clear in his mind

was the exact moment he'd reached his first climax with her while thrusting into her repeatedly, liking the way her inner muscles had clamped tight around him, holding him in their grip, milking everything out of him and—

"Now you're getting bigger."

Her voice sliced through his thoughts. Then with full awareness of what was taking place, he tightened his legs, keeping her in a fixed position beside him. "I know," he said huskily, unable to stop what was about to happen yet again.

He heard her suck in a trembling breath, watched as her eyes darkened to the point where he could barely see the long lashes covering them. But he was able to make out the expression on her face. There was something about seeing the look of an aroused woman, especially a totally naked one.

He reached out and rubbed the tip of his finger around her belly button. His caress didn't alter when he heard the sharp change in her breathing pattern or when he felt the slight quivering of her thighs beneath his.

"What are you doing to me?" she asked softly, barely able to enunciate any of the words.

Hearing the lack of comprehension in her voice endeared her to him even more. He figured that he could show her better than tell her. Leaning forward, he came within inches of her lips. "Um, what do you think I'm doing?" he asked, as he softly stroked the flat planes of her stomach with his fingertips.

"I—I can't think," she whispered, closing her eyes on a throaty sigh.

"Then don't. Just feel."

And then he began moving, excruciatingly slow, deep inside her, gradually withdrawing, then filling her again, deeper still in a leisurely measured thrusting motion. He felt sensations sear through the both of them from such a long, drawn-out and unhurried mating process.

"Open your eyes, Taylor," he whispered in a raspy voice, as he continued to thrust slowly in and out of her, savoring each and every time he did so.

He watched as she did what he asked, met her gaze mere seconds before he leaned closer and took her mouth. The stroke of his tongue with hers was as slow and deliberate as the mating of their bodies— surging forward, retreating and then surging forward again.

Then something inside him snapped and without disconnecting from her, he shifted his body astride her, crossed her leg over his in a scissors position, allowing deeper penetration with her being the one in control using her thighs. It was different from the more common lovemaking positions because all four of their legs were intercrossed. He had seen this particular position in the book but was well familiar with "cuissade," which derived from the French. It was a position he had first used with a woman the year he'd turned eighteen when his parents had sent him to spend the summer in Paris with his father's childhood friend Jacques Gaston and his family. The Gastons' young, sexually active housekeeper had been more than happy to visit his room every night when her employers were asleep. He had received quite an education that summer.

Not wanting to think of anything other than the woman in his arms, Dominic lowered his head and kissed Taylor at the same time he slowly began moving in and out of her again. He could feel his erection expanding inside her with each gentle thrust he took.

She suddenly pulled her mouth away from him. "Dominic!"

He felt her muscles tighten around him and clench him in an unwavering grip. Her thighs began to quiver uncontrollably and due to the deliberate pressure of her thighs on his legs, the motion had the ability to shake him to the core. Sensations began spurting through him, eliciting his own torrid release. He felt the full impact of their orgasm in every part of his body.

"Taylor," he said in a guttural groan before leaning over and kissing her while simultaneously releasing inside her the life-creating substance that would produce a baby.

His baby.

Their baby.

Never before had he wanted such a thing to happen more than he did now. He released her mouth and reached out and placed a gentle hand on her stomach as if willing it so. She gazed up at him, as if understanding the meaning of what he was doing. The possibility that she was perceptive enough to interpret his thoughts had a nerve-tingling effect on him.

For a fraction of a second, he just stared at her, feeling the heated flush of their connected bodies. It was nothing short of pure, raw sexual pleasure. And as he eased his body to lie beside her, still not ready to pull out of her, he looked forward to the next time they would make love.

"Thank you for calling room service and asking that they deliver our dinner at a more convenient time," Taylor said after taking a sip of her iced tea. It was harder than she thought it would be to sit across from Dominic and attempt to eat a full-course meal. Each and every time his gaze touched her, she would feel the potent, invisible caress all over her body, making her remember what the two of them had shared in the bedroom.

"I think they understood, since we weren't the only couple who postponed dinner to later," Dominic said, pushing his plate back.

Taylor watched the gesture and swallowed deeply.

It had been but a couple of hours since they'd last made love yet he wanted her again. The realization sent a shiver down her spine, because she wanted him, too. She picked up the tea glass and looked at it. The server had blatantly told them that it was plum tea, known as the ultimate erotic energizer. She believed him. After taking only a few sips she had felt a surge in her pulse, a pull in her belly and a throb between her legs. She'd thought a full stomach would rectify the problem but it hadn't.

Still, she took another sip of the tea, knowing it was coursing through her bloodstream, releasing something she really didn't need, considering her and Dominic's actions of earlier. All he had to do was look at her and she felt the need to jump his bones. After making love that last time they had fallen asleep, only to wake up and make love again. Four times in one evening was definitely setting a record for her.

"Did you want to watch that movie later?"

She glanced over at him. "What movie?"

"The one the resort suggested that all the couples watch."

Oh, that movie. Her heart began thumping at what the movie was probably about. "Do you think we need to watch it?"

He chuckled. "No, but we might find it interesting."

She was pretty certain they would. "I'll do whatever you want to do," she decided.

He met her gaze. "What if I told you I wanted to clear this table and take you right on top of it?"

A vision of such a thing happening immediately speared through her mind and had hot blood rushing through her veins. "Would you really want to do that?"

"Yes." He didn't miss a beat in responding. "You would be my dessert, Taylor."

He was giving her a wicked smile but she knew he was dead serious. She could feel her muscles weaken, her insides tremble. She also knew he was getting her hot and bothered on purpose. They were sitting across from each other wearing the resort's complimentary bathrobes without a stitch of clothing underneath. It wouldn't be hard to do what he'd suggested. In fact it would be downright easy with the way she was feeling.

She leaned forward knowing she was exposing a little of her cleavage in the process since her robe wasn't pulled tightly together. "I've never been taken on a table before but I don't want my first time to be planned. I want it to be spontaneous. I want it to just happen."

"Okay."

He had agreed as if such a thing happening wouldn't pose a problem. "I like surprises," she decided to add.

"You also enjoy giving surprises," he said, taking a sip of his own tea. "I wasn't expecting that sexy red number you put on earlier."

She smiled, pleased she had caught him off guard. "Yes, I know."

"I owe you one."

She wanted to tell him he had already delivered four times tonight, but decided she shouldn't be counting, although she was. "I'm looking forward to payback time."

Another smile touched his lips. "So, do we do the movie?"

She met his gaze. It was either do the movie or do each other and she figured their bodies needed a time-out period. "Yes, we do the movie."

Dominic glanced at the clock on the wall. The movie titled *A Hot Winter's Night* was to start in about fifteen minutes. He was sitting at one end of the sofa with Taylor at the other. He inwardly chuckled at the thought that they had unconsciously placed distance between them and he knew why. If they got any closer they would end up not watching the movie.

He couldn't release from his mind the thought of the time he had made love to her using the cuissade position with slow, elicit detail. He had been able to stare into her face, see each and every passionate response. He had held back from taking her fast and hard, much preferring to savor each and every thrust. There was another particular position he wanted to try with her before the week was out and he felt his erection throb at the thought.

"Tell me some more about your family," he said, to pass the time and to get making love to her again off his mind…for now.

She glanced over at him. "What do you want to know?"

He shrugged. "Anything you want to tell me."

So she began talking, and he listened…at least he tried to. But it was hard while observing the movement of her breasts when she used her hands when talking. Whenever she moved her hands her breasts would stick out, press against the fabric of the robe. Watching it made him want to ease over her and remove the robe from her and then take his mouth and have his way with not only her breasts, but every inch of her. That was something he hadn't done yet. Taste her. His tongue was more than anxious for that to happen.

"Dominic?"

Her saying his name got his attention. "Yes?"

"I've finished telling you about my family and was asking you to tell me about yours." She smiled. "You obviously weren't paying attention."

He laughed. "Obviously." He leaned back against the sofa. "So what do you want to know?"

"Anything you want to tell me since my baby will be a Saxon. Any aunts and uncles? Grandparents?"

He shook his head. "No, neither of my parents have siblings." And because he didn't consider himself as having a grandparent, he said, "And no grandparents, either. I do have godparents, though."

He then told her about the Gastons. In the middle of the conversation the movie started and all talking between them ceased as their attention was drawn to the big television screen in front of them.

Taylor bit the insides of her lip as she stared at the television screen. The movie was as erotic as it could get. It definitely had to be X-rated or possibly double X-rated. The first time a love scene had flashed on she'd actually blushed watching it with Dominic. He, on the other hand, seemed pretty relaxed and at some point had stretched his legs out into a more comfortable position. But he had remained on his end of the sofa and she on hers. However, even with distance between them, seeing the naked actors and actresses hadn't stopped heat from traveling up her spine or her imagining her and Dominic in the starring roles.

"Do you know why the resort wanted us to watch this tonight?" he broke into the silence between them to ask.

She figured he knew the answer but wanted to hear her opinion. "Because it's sexually explicit imagery, designed to stimulate."

He glanced over at her. "Is it?"

Her eyebrows pressed together. "Is it what?"

"Stimulating you?"

She shrugged. "Somewhat. I guess seeing two sexy people on a screen making out would stimulate most since it shows variety, new ideas and different positions."

She glanced over at him. "Is it stimulating you?"

"Yes."

Suddenly the television screen went black and it was then that she noted he held the remote in his hand. She wanted to think "typical male" but she knew there wasn't anything typical about Dominic.

"Slide over here for a minute, Taylor."

She swallowed deeply as she met his gaze. Emotions swirled within her at the desire he wasn't trying to hide in his eyes. "Why?" she asked, barely able to get the single word out.

"Because I want you over here with me right now."

She heard the tenseness in his voice and for a long, endless moment, she didn't say anything, and then, "Is it necessary?"

"Trust me on this, Taylor. It is."

She had been watching the television as he'd been doing and recalled what had been playing before it had gone black. The couple had been making out on the sofa, performing oral sex on each other.

He was still staring at her when she finally slid over toward him, coming to sit directly next to him. With a throaty chuckle and not knowing what to expect, she said, "Well, here I am."

He leaned his face closer to hers. "I want you even closer."

She felt sizzling heat flow through her veins. "If I get any closer, Dominic, I'll be in your lap."

He gave her a sexy smile. "Yeah, I know." And then he reached out and lifted her into his lap. She quickly realized the enormous size of his erection. It was protruding hard against her bottom. She placed her arm around his neck, which made her bathrobe gape open. Before she had a chance to pull it back together, Dominic's hands were there. "No, let it stay open," he said in a deep, husky voice.

The warmth of his touch on her skin sent shivers down her spine. He then leaned closer and gently dropped his head in the center of her chest and brushed a kiss there. Then she felt a flick of his tongue and a lick in that very spot. She could feel the area between her legs getting wet. So easily and just that quickly.

He suddenly shifted positions and she felt herself gently being pushed back against the sofa's cushions with him looming over her. He had stretched her out on the sofa and had gotten on his knees beside it. "I think reality is much better than sitting here watching a movie," he said, reaching out and completely opening her robe.

Taylor couldn't restrain the heat from suffusing her body when Dominic's gaze roamed over her nakedness. And as she stared at him she saw his eyes darken even more and detected the exact moment his breathing changed.

He lifted his gaze and looked at her. "I think I'm becoming addicted."

She paused mentally as she took in what he'd said. Would his addiction extend beyond the week they would share here together? They really hadn't made any ground rules. She'd just assumed he understood that anything beyond this week was not a possibility. She had to start planning her life around a baby and she was sure his schedule was just as demanding. He traveled a lot. He had a lot on his plate. From what she'd read in the magazines, his affairs were more misses than hits, intentionally so on his part. He liked affairs. She didn't have time for even that much of a relationship. The only reason she had carved out this week was because more than anything she wanted a baby. Not a full-time or part-time lover.

Any thoughts were suddenly snatched from Taylor's mind when she felt Dominic's fingers settle between her legs. She recalled what had happened the last time he had touched her there. With the skill of his fingers, it wasn't long before he had her entire body trembling. There was no doubt in her mind that his intimate touch was being branded on her brain. Sensations were drumming through her and she dug her teeth into her lower lip to stop from screaming out.

She met his gaze and saw the heated lust that darkened his eyes and knew they had to be a mirror of hers. He was deliberately taunting her feminine core, making her want him to the point where she was almost ready to beg.

"You're extremely wet, Taylor," he said in a low, throaty voice as he continued to stroke her with expert precision. "Your heated scent is powerful, intoxicating and arousing. Do you know what I want to do?"

Make love to her, she hoped. *Now.* He was looking at her expectantly since he had asked her a question. Was he really expecting an answer? She doubted her mind could form coherent words to give him one. Instead she pushed herself to say, "No, what do you want to do?"

"Taste you."

When he lowered his head between her legs it hit her that he hadn't been asking permission. He was taking what he wanted. And when his tongue flicked out and gave her that first intimate touch, she felt boneless; pleasure of the most intense kind seeped through her pores.

"Dominic." She closed her eyes on a blissful sigh as he continued to kiss her in the most intimate way a man could. Even while part of her mind was telling her to resist him—to reach out and jerk his head up—the only thing she could do was reach out and grab hold of his head to hold it in place.

But the reality of it was that it didn't look as though he planned to go anywhere anytime soon. He was assaulting her with thorough, leisurely strokes of his tongue, relentless in his actions. And she was unashamedly enjoying it.

She became aware of the shiver that raced through her body, and his tongue probed deeper, becoming more demanding, greedier. She let out an intense moan from deep within her throat. Her hands holding his head tightened as if to draw him closer and he continued going at her as if her taste was something he just had to have.

Her body exploded, seemingly into a thousand pieces, and she let out a high-pitched scream as deep gratification seared through her with the impact of concrete hitting steel. She realized his hold on her was just as immobilizing as her hold on him. He had a firm grip on her thighs, not intending to let her go anyplace until he'd gotten his fill, and that thought sent her over the edge again.

Never in her life had anything happened to her like this before. Not only this time, but all those other times tonight with Dominic. This just wasn't normal for her and she wondered if it would have been normal for any woman. She suddenly had a fleeting thought that continuing beyond this week wouldn't be bad if she got to experience something like this. Her job could be stressful and making love to Dominic could certainly take the edge off things.

She finally felt her body floating back to Earth when Dominic lifted his mouth from her. He raised his head to stare down at her while licking his lips in the process, and the gesture was so erotic she reached out and pulled his mouth to hers. She tasted herself on his lips, his tongue, leaving her with no doubt of how intense his intimate kiss had been.

And then she felt her body being lifted into his strong arms and knew they would finish what they had started in the bedroom.

Dominic stood at the window and looked out at the ocean. It was dark outside yet he could see the waves hitting the shore. He turned slightly to glance at the clock on the nightstand. It was almost two in the morning. Taylor was still sleeping. He, however, had gotten out of bed after finding it impossible to sleep. So here he was, standing at the window gazing out into the night. It was either that or wake up Taylor to make love again.

Sheesh. He had made love to her more times in one night than he had to any woman in such a short span of time. He tried convincing himself not to be bothered by that statistic since to make love was the reason they were here, and the more times they did it the better the chances of her getting pregnant. He could accept that. But what he didn't want to accept was just how much he was enjoying it. Not that he thought he wouldn't. He just hadn't figured on doing so to this extreme—especially not to the point where his erection hadn't gone down any over the past twelve hours or so. That was simply remarkable.

He shook his head thinking that no, *that* was Taylor.

The woman had the ability to excite him by doing the smallest things. Hell, just looking at any part of her body made him want her, and to think they had six more days to go. If they kept going at it the rate they were doing now, by the end of the seventh day the hotel staff would have to come in with a crowbar to pry their bodies apart.

He rubbed his hand down his face thinking that come morning they needed to get out of the hotel room for a while and take a tour of the island or something. Anything that would get them out of their suite. Taylor was becoming one hell of a temptation.

None of the brochures had mentioned any outside activities since the sole purpose of the procreation vacation was focused on a single activity that was mainly done indoors. But still, if necessary, he was ready to take drastic measures since what he'd told Taylor earlier was true. He was becoming addicted to her and that thought didn't sit well with him. In fact, it was beginning to annoy the hell out of him. It wasn't his intent to become obsessed with any woman to the point that he couldn't walk away when he was good and ready, and without any lingering thoughts. Taylor was making it hard as hell to consider doing so.

Deciding he needed a definite plan before she woke up, he moved away from the window and grabbed his shirt and pants off a nearby chair. Within minutes he was heading out the door to talk to the person at the front desk.

The moment he stepped into the elevator he wished he hadn't. There was no doubt in his mind what he'd come within mere seconds of catching the couple doing. The woman was quickly getting off her knees and the man was turning his back to him to rezip his pants. Dominic wasn't sure who was the more embarrassed, so he stared at the elevator door as though he was oblivious to everything and was glad when the elevator came to the lobby. Since the couple made no move to get off, he could only assume they intended to continue what they were doing before his interruption and this time he hoped they had the good sense to stop the elevators between floors.

Glad at the moment that he no longer had a boner, he walked briskly over to the check-in desk. An older man looked up, seemingly surprised to see him or anyone up and about at that time of morning. "Yes, sir, may I help you?"

"I hope you can. Is there anything else around here to do?"

The man, who appeared to be in his late fifties, gave him a strange look as if to say, *the main thing around here takes place in the bedroom and you obviously aren't there.* However, he merely said, "It depends on what you want do."

"What I want to do," Dominic heard himself say, "is something that will take me and my wife away from the resort for a few hours."

The man looked appalled. "You want to leave your suite?"

Dominic couldn't help but smile. This man evidently took the resort's ability to produce results—specifically those that came nine months from now—pretty seriously. "Yes, just for a few hours but don't worry, this place is definitely living up to our expectations."

A relieved expression appeared on the man's face when he said, "Thank you, sir, and we do have a couple of activities outside the resort that some of our visitors seem to enjoy on occasion. We can arrange for you to rent a sailboat, and then there's horseback riding along the beach, a private picnic at one of the remote cottages and—"

"I like the idea of going sailing," he quickly said, deciding he didn't need him and Taylor going anywhere slightly remote. "Make the necessary arrangements, and since we'll probably be gone past lunch, I think a picnic lunch would be nice."

"Certainly, sir. I'll take care of everything for you."

Chapter 7

Taylor slowly opened her eyes and saw Dominic sitting in one of the chairs across from the bed. He appeared bigger than life and was definitely impossible to miss. The sunlight shining through the window was beaming on him at an angle that made her insides flutter. He was an incredibly attractive man.

She shifted in bed and the ache she felt in certain muscles quickly reminded her that he was also a skillful lover—and she hoped a very potent one. After their passionate encounters last night she was pretty convinced she was probably pregnant already. But they had six days and nights to go.

"Good morning."

At the sound of his voice she forcibly put those thoughts to the back of her mind. She was still having delicious aftershocks of last night and seeing him sitting lazily in the chair with his legs stretched out in front of him wasn't helping matters. At least he was fully dressed.

"Good morning," she said, pulling herself up in bed, making sure she kept a tight grip on the bedspread covering her. He might be dressed but she was still completely naked. So much for all those nightgowns she had brought along. At the rate they were going she wouldn't be using them. At least she'd had on the red one for a split second before he'd taken it off her.

"How would you like to go sailing today?"

The low, sexy tone of his voice had tiny little shivers moving down her spine. "Sailing?"

"Yes."

It would get them out of the suite for a while, she thought, and couldn't help wondering if that was the reason he'd come up with the idea. Was he getting tired of her already?

"Trust me, that's not it."

She blinked. "Excuse me?"

He eased his tall frame from the chair and came to stand beside the bed. She thought he looked simply gorgeous in a pair of jeans and a blue polo shirt. "I saw something flash in your eyes just now that I've never seen before. Not in all the time I've known you," he said softly.

She bit her lip nervously. "What?"

"Doubt. And you're one of the most confident people I know, male or female. The only reason I think it's best that we remove ourselves from this suite for a while is because if we don't, we're liable to try every damn position in that book and there're close to sixty of them."

She couldn't help the smile that touched her lips. "Sixty-five to be exact."

There was an electric silence in the room as if they were both remembering the ones they had tried so far. "I'll leave so you can get dressed," Dominic finally said, as he turned toward the door.

"I thought you said you wouldn't be taking any more showers alone," she couldn't help but say.

He stopped walking and turned back around. The look he gave her was filled with desire, as if it wouldn't take much for him to cross the room and strip her naked. "Trust me. It took all I had not to wake you when I took mine, but the next time I won't spare any mercy. I plan to have you in there with me."

His eyes challenged her to deny what he'd said as a fact and she couldn't. Doing so would be point-less. In just one night she had discovered she enjoyed making love with him way too much. The man was too downright irresistible for his own good…and hers. She had never responded to another man the way she was responding to him.

The moment he closed the door behind him, she eased out of bed, hoping he wouldn't change his mind and decide to join her in the shower anyway. She moved around the bedroom gathering up everything she would need for her bath and trying to decide which of the outfits she'd brought along would be appropriate for sailing. She placed her underthings on the bed and before going into the bathroom she strolled to the window and looked out. She was again in awe at the beauty of the island. The ocean looked inviting and she would enjoy being out on it in a sailboat.

Moments later she stepped under a jet of warm water thinking a shower was what she needed for her sore muscles because they had definitely been put to the test. The last time when they'd made love before finally drifting off to sleep, they had used another position from that book. A smile formed on her lips. The leapfrog position definitely had had its merits.

Deciding she needed to get dressed quickly before Dominic was tempted to come find out what was taking her so long, she turned off the water and stepped out of the shower and began toweling dry with one of the huge fluffy towels. Once she was dry she wrapped the towel around her before making her way back to the bedroom to select something out of her closet.

She found an outfit she thought would be perfect,

a pair of crochet-trim gauchos with a matching tunic top that tied at the back of the neck. It was an outfit she had purchased last summer while visiting Cheyenne in Jamaica.

Moments later she stood, completely dressed in front of the mirror, viewing the results and finding them acceptable. She hoped when Dominic saw her he would like the results, as well. One thing she noticed was that with the style of the outfit, several passion marks were blatantly visible. A shiver passed through her. She could recall the exact moment each and every single one was made. Dominic had made sure of it.

She took a deep breath as she glanced at the unmade bed and could actually feel her body beginning to throb with the memories of last night. The thought that she could even now be pregnant filled her with intense pleasure as she walked to the door.

"If I didn't know better, Dominic, I'd think you were a born seaman."

Dominic glanced over at Taylor, his gaze roaming over her from behind dark aviator sunglasses. He liked the outfit she had chosen to wear and thought that she looked sexy in it. She was leaning against the ship's railing with the sun in the background, seemingly shining directly on her. It was a perfect day to be out on the water and he was glad she was out here with him.

His mind shifted back to her comment and he decided not to tell her that in essence he really was a born seaman. The Saxons of France had made their fortune in the shipping industry for centuries and his father had been taught to navigate a water-craft before learning to walk. If you bothered to dig up the family history, the Saxons had been and always would be men of the sea. Marcello Saxon had passed his love for the ocean on to him and Dominic intended to pass that love on to his son or daughter. Some of his fondest memories were of the times when his father had routinely taken Dominic and his mother with him on his father's first luxury cruise liners.

"How are you feeling?" he asked her, more out of genuine concern than a way to change the sub-ject. He hadn't missed the fact that her steps were a lot slower today and he knew why. She knew why, too, which he figured was the reason a blush ap-peared in her face.

"I'm fine," she answered and turned to look back over the ocean.

He smiled. After all they'd shared last night, every single thing they'd done, how on earth could she get embarrassed by his question? He was dis-covering a lot about his wealth and asset manger turned temporary lover. He knew she was allergic to certain types of nuts, had a tendency to over-indulge in chocolate and loved watching scary movies. And in the past hour, with his encouragement, she had shared more about her family with him. There was no doubt in his mind the Steeles were close. She admired her male cousins and thought the world of her two sisters.

It had always been his parents' wish to have another child but miscarriages before and after his birth made them change their minds and decide he would be the one and only. Listening to Taylor made him realize that, other than Matt, he hadn't had a lot of friends or family while growing up. He had been sent to private schools most of his life, some outside the United Sates. And after that kidnapping attempt, it was a long time before his parents or Ryder would let him out of their sight.

"Hungry yet?" he decided to ask her.

She turned, lifted a brow and smiled. "What if I am? It's not like we're going to find a restaurant out here."

He gave a soft laugh. "No, but we do have that," he said, nodding to the huge picnic basket she hadn't yet seen near the bow.

She followed his gaze and smiled. "Who brought that on?"

"The management of the resort," he said. "I ordered lunch for us when I requested the boat. I'm ready to eat when you are."

She smiled. "Okay then, I'm ready."

* * *

"Wow, the resort really did it up, didn't they?" Taylor said while watching Dominic unload the picnic basket. There were numerous sandwiches, a platter of cheeses, bags of chips, a container of fruit, a Thermos filled with coffee and a bottle of chilled nonalcoholic wine.

"Um, I specifically told them about the nonalcoholic wine just in case you're in a delicate condition already. And since I'm the captain of this vessel, I can't drink on the job," he said, putting the empty basket aside to pour wine into their glasses. "I have to make sure we get back to land safely before nightfall."

Taylor grinned. "And I appreciate that." She placed the plate filled with food in her lap. Dominic had done the serving and had given her a little bit of everything.

She glanced over at him. "So, what kind of kid were you while growing up, so I can know what to expect?"

He threw his head back and laughed. "It might be too late to determine that, isn't it? It wouldn't surprise me any if you're pregnant already."

She had thought the same thing but to hear him say it out loud made goose bumps appear on her arms. "Too bad there's no way we can find out."

"I don't want to know," he said, taking a sip of his wine.

She lifted a brow. "Why?"

He met her gaze over the glass. "If you knew you were pregnant already then you wouldn't need for us to stay the remainder of the week. Just think of all the fun we'd miss out on."

She was thinking. But then she knew that eventually all good things came to an end. "So tell me," she encouraged. "What kind of child were you? Spoiled I bet."

A small smile touched his lips. "I guess there was a little of that since I was the only child, but I knew just how far to go in riling my parents. I didn't have any siblings or a bunch of cousins like you have, but I had Matt."

"Matt?"

"Yes, Matt Caulder. He's my attorney and best friend. Our mothers were childhood friends, and in a way Matt and I were raised together. Then his mother died of breast cancer. It was our final year of high school. That was a difficult time for him."

"I can imagine," she said, thinking of the time she had lost her father while in high school, as well. "I know how he felt. I lost Dad while in high school, too. He died of lung cancer."

"Was he a smoker?"

"Yes, of the worst kind. We tried to get him to quit and never could." She was silent for a few minutes. "So tell me about Matt. Is he married?" she asked curiously.

Dominic shook his head. "Divorced. Unfortunately things didn't work out. But he'll be quick to tell you the best thing to come from his marriage was Dee—short for Deena. She's his two-year-old daughter and was named after his mother. I'm her godfather. I've got pictures. You want to see?"

"Sure."

Taylor watched as Dominic put aside his plate to pull out his wallet. He would make a wonderful father, she thought, and a sense of pride touched her in knowing his child would be hers.

She took the photograph he handed to her. Dee was definitely a pretty little girl. "She's blessed to have both you and her father in her life," Taylor said as she continued looking at the picture. "It's important for little girls, as well as little boys, to have strong male role models."

"Yes, it is," he agreed.

Taylor handed him back the photograph and their hands touched. The sensation that hit the both of them, simultaneously, made their breaths catch. Her eyes flew to his face. "Sorry about that," she said apologetically.

"It's not your fault," he said, intentionally not looking at her while placing Dee's picture back in his wallet.

No, and neither was it his, she thought. It seemed they were two irresistible forces that attracted, even when they weren't trying to. They couldn't help it.

Weren't strong enough to stop it. Even now there was a sexually charged awareness between the two of them. The very air they were breathing seemed electrified, sensually combustible.

For the next few moments they ate in silence. That gave her a chance to look around and check out the sailboat. It was a beauty with nice accommodations. While he had been busy getting ready to sail, she had gone below to check out things. There were a number of screened ports as well as multiple overhead hatches intended to circulate fresh air. What had caught her eye was the queen-size berth in the aft stateroom, as well as the built-in lounge seat and hanging lockers. The bathroom was small but contained a shower with hot and cold water, a sink and vanity. Also below was a highly styled gourmet galley with a beautifully detailed teak interior.

When they had boarded, Dominic had said something about it being large enough to sleep six people and that the size of the boat eliminated a lot of rocking. She had to agree since so far it had been smooth sailing. He was the captain and she smiled, remembering that he had made her his mate. After bringing the boat into the wind, he had asked her to hold the wheel while he lowered the sail. She had enjoyed doing that. It had made her feel useful and a part of what he was doing.

She tilted her face up toward the sun, thinking

there was a nice breeze in the air and all she could see for miles around was ocean. They had left any semblance of land behind hours ago. It seemed they were the only two people at that moment under a glorious blue sky.

Out of the corner of her eye she saw Dominic move and she turned her head and watched him. He was standing up and looking out at the sea. Before leaving the resort, he had swapped his jeans for a pair of denim shorts, and as he stood there with his legs braced apart, his shoulders bracketed against the wind and his hands jammed into the pockets of his shorts it was obvious that he was definitely a gorgeous specimen of a man. And with the sun and ocean in the background surrounding him, he looked totally at ease. Even from where she sat she could feel the sexual tension within him and it was having an effect on her. It was stirring things within her. The need she felt for him was poignant, keen and cutting sharp. It was weakening her with desire.

He suddenly turned and met her gaze. The atmosphere seemed even more stimulated. Her breath caught when she felt it. It was like fire seeping through her veins. It prickled her skin, sharpened her senses and created a relentless throb between her legs.

"I tried," he finally spoke and said grimly. But at the same time she heard an edge in his voice.

"And what have you tried?" she asked, thinking

maybe it was better if she didn't know but desperately wanting to.

"I tried not to want you as much today."

She nodded then gave him a curious look. "And why not today?" she queried softly.

He gave her a tense look. "Because I had you too much yesterday."

He said it as if that should explain things. It didn't. "Considering the reason we're here, Dominic, there are no limitations. It's all you can get."

He smiled. "If that were true then I'd keep you on your back with only bathroom breaks."

The image of that flowed through her mind, made the throb between her legs intensify. "But it is true. We came to make a baby. Don't worry about wearing me out. I can handle it. This is one case where the means will justify the results."

She didn't say anything for a second and then she couldn't help but ask, "Why are you fighting it?

Taylor's words hung in the air, refusing to float away, Dominic thought. She had just asked him a loaded question. How could he explain that the reason he was fighting it was because he felt himself getting too emotionally attached? And that when he was making love to her, he felt things he hadn't felt with any woman. She was right. He was furiously trying to fight it and the sad part was that he couldn't. She had the ability to stir up things inside him. It was beginning to irritate the hell out of him that she was becoming his weakness, something he didn't have time for. Weak men became vulnerable men. They became men who couldn't think straight. Men who let their guard down.

"Dominic?"

She was waiting on his response but there was no answer he could truthfully give her. Instead he said, "I'm not fighting it. I thought I was being a gentleman and trying not to give the impression that I'm a greedy ass who enjoys being inside you 24-7."

"But I love having you inside me. Because I know the reason why you're there."

To make a baby, he contemplated roughly, wondering why he was getting upset at the thought that, as she said, he was just a means to an end. "Do you know what you're asking for?"

"Yes. I knew it the moment I arrived on the island. Even before that. I also knew that because I hadn't been sexually active in quite some time that the first couple of days wouldn't be easy for me, they would probably be uncomfortable. But my body is adjusting. I'm fine."

Dominic heard her words. He also saw how the sun was playing across the beauty of her features. His glance then moved slowly over her entire body and suddenly, he didn't want to talk anymore. He wanted to do what he'd been fighting all day.

There were no other boats around. It was as if

they were in their own private world. There was no shoreline in sight. It was just the two of them and the wide-open span of the Atlantic Ocean. More than anything he wanted to make love to her here, on the deck, under the sun. Right this minute. But then he thought of her comfort.

"Will you go down below with me?" he asked silkily, more than sure she knew the reason he was asking.

She didn't hesitate when she responded. "Yes."

Taylor's breath quickened at the way Dominic was looking at her. She knew why he wanted to take her below and the thought of making love with him on the open seas made hot blood rush through her veins.

Determined not to give him a chance or a reason to change his mind, she walked over to him. When she came to stand in front of him, she said, "I've never made love on a boat before."

The look he was giving her made her skin tingle. "Then your first time will be special. I'll make sure of that." He swung her up into his arms.

Somehow he managed to get the both of them below and placed her on the bed. Once her body touched the mattress, she didn't want them to waste any more time and began removing her clothes, beginning with her top.

"No, please let me."

She glanced up when Dominic moved closer to

the bed and reached out his hand to pull her to him. Then his arms folded around her and he simply stood there for a second holding her in his warm embrace. His manly aroma teased her nostrils and her stomach began to quiver. Moments later, he leaned back and met her gaze and the look she saw in his eyes let her know there wouldn't be time for any small talk. The idea of that made her pulse leap, her heart beat fast and furious in her chest. Then he began removing the rest of her clothes, taking his time as a cooling breeze came through the screened porthole and touched her naked skin.

When she was completely naked, his gaze moved over her, taking its time and lingering on those marks of passion that were still there. "I've branded you," he whispered as a satisfied smile curved his lips.

Taylor swallowed, thinking he had done a lot more than that. There was no way she would tell him how she felt at this very moment. What was between them was an agreement, one as personal as it could get; however, things were to have remained unemotional. But it seemed whenever they came together like this, things were as emotional as they could get.

"Now I want to undress you," she said softly, reaching out and lifting up Dominic's shirt over his head. When she had removed it, she tossed it aside and went to the snaps of his shorts. He was aroused, she noted when she eased down his zipper. His manhood was huge, she saw when he stepped away from the bed to remove his shoes. And when he eased his shorts and briefs together down his thighs, she saw that he was also extremely ready. The size of him no longer bothered her as it had that first night. Her body had been able to take him right in.

He came back to the bed. "I want to try something different," he stated huskily.

She tilted her head back and met his gaze. "What?"

"I want you to ride me."

He had thumbed through that book as many times as she had, and he knew that the "woman on top" position was the least effective to use to get her pregnant, due to the law of gravity. But it was a position that she knew gave the woman the most pleasure because it placed her in a dominating role. She understood what Dominic was doing. He wanted them to make love for the sheer enjoyment of doing so, not for the sole purpose of making a baby.

A part of her wasn't sure she was ready for what he was asking. It would add a piece to the equation that she hadn't counted on. Even doing what he asked only one time would still throw a monkey wrench into their week here. She had a tendency to let herself go when they made love and had convinced herself she was only doing so because each time they came together, there was a chance they were creating a life—a life they both wanted. What if she let herself go anyway? What if he still had the ability to rock her world although he was placing her in control?

She had to fight hard to retain her composure. Just being here with him, sitting naked in the middle of the bed, staring into the deep green of his eyes was rocking her world, slinging her into an arena of emotions and feelings she hadn't counted on, nor was prepared for. He was unshaven and the mass of hair on his head was tousled around his shoulders. Her gaze raked over his face and her breathing quickened when her eyes lowered to move across his manly chest and then down past his waist to his huge manhood that was fully erect in a bed of dark curly hair.

And she knew at that moment that yes, she would ride him. The need to do so had become an ache in her belly. There was no other position that could remove it and an abundance of rising excitement filled her entire being.

"Taylor?"

She moved her gaze back up to his face. She saw the intensity in the dark pupils staring straight at her. She felt the heat and the potent force of his sexuality. It was dominant, overbearing and lethal, and it was reaching out to her, touching her in some of the most private places. Instead of giving him an answer, she eased toward him and reached up and wrapped her arms around his neck. She studied his lips and thought his mouth was temptation at its finest, and with a gentle pull he was tumbling down on the bed with her.

Their mouths connected immediately and she began drowning in his heat the moment their tongues connected. And knowing just where their kiss would lead kicked a response in her that went beyond anything she'd ever encountered before.

And then he was shifting their bodies to place her on top and she pulled back and stared down at him.

She wanted him.

Her arms grabbed hold of his shoulders and she felt his muscles tighten beneath her fingertips. She felt his manhood in the center of her legs and it was a struggle not to lower her body onto it. However, temptation made her lean down and take a swipe of his lips with her tongue. His sharp intake of breath made her smile.

"I think I'd better warn you that I took horseback riding as a child," she informed him softly.

He continued to look at her and lifted a brow. "And?"

She chuckled. "And I'm no novice. I like riding."

She saw the way his eyes darkened. She felt the way his hard length seemed to thicken beneath her. Then suddenly he gripped her hips and lifted them enough to position his shaft at the opening of her womanly core. She felt the tip of its head right there. "I like riding, too," he said in a strained voice, lowering her hips downward to inch inside her.

She felt the heat of him, big and thick, as it entered her, stretching her body again to accommodate its presence. He continued to lower her onto him and she could barely breathe at the feeling of him filling her so completely.

She felt the exact moment he lifted the lower part of his body off the bed to drive into her to the hilt. "Let's ride," he growled from deep in his throat.

He had told her to ride him, not to kill him, Dominic thought as Taylor's body slammed down on his once more, pressing her knees into his sides, holding firm to his shoulders. Her head was thrown back and she was giving the bed one hell of a workout while at the same time driving his body over the edge, time and time again.

He'd come twice already and so had she, but she wouldn't let up and he couldn't seem to go down. She was doing more than just rocking the bed. She was also rocking his senses, tilting his world, filling him with more pleasure than he could have imagined possible. He'd heard of women who were experts when it came to riding, but until now he'd never encountered one. The sheer impact of how she was making him feel simply overwhelmed him. And the scent of sex along with the fragrance of her perfume wasn't helping matters when he inhaled it into his nostrils. It only made him that much more aware of what they were doing and how they were doing it. And the knowledge that they were out in the middle of the ocean only added to the allure, the deep throb in his veins and the degree of his arousal that wouldn't go away.

She kept going and going and going, as if working up to that one big explosion that would be the granddaddy of them all. So each time she came down on him, he was there to thrust up into her, grind his body, going as deep inside her as he could, and the more he did so, the more vigorously she bucked and pumped into him, going at it wild and untamed.

He felt another climax ready to hit him at the same moment he felt her inner body clench his muscles and felt this release would be too good to waste, so he quickly shifted positions and brought her beneath him the moment her body jerked. She let out one hair-raising scream when she exploded. He followed her and flooded her insides with the very essence of him, and held her, refusing to let her move, wanting her to feel what he'd done. Take it all in. Keep it.

Her response didn't help and when she wrapped her legs around him, locking him in, he continued to kiss her—harder—while slipping his hands into her hair to grip the silkiness of it and to hold her mouth in place. She was being held hostage, under his intense desire.

He knew that he was being held hostage under hers, as well.

Chapter 8

Taylor felt Dominic's touch when he slid his hand between her legs, gently stroking her there. He was lying beside her, facing her, and when her lips parted with a soft purr he leaned forward and took advantage, letting his tongue begin an intimate dance inside her mouth that only he had the skill to perform. Feeling like putty in his hands, under his lips, she clung to his mouth in a kiss of possession that she felt all the way to her toes.

Moments later, he released her mouth and whispered softly against her moist lips. "You okay?"

She was also too absorbed in the sensual spell he had placed her in to speak. She felt totally drained in a way that still had parts of her body quivering. Even now there was a heated pulse between her legs in the area where he was stroking.

"Yes, I'm fine," she whispered back, filled with an emotional need she didn't want, but was too weak to resist. Each time she made love with him she felt herself being pulled in toward something she wasn't sure had a name, but was certain didn't have a place in her life. She didn't like things getting complicated. The only thing she wanted from Dominic was the one thing she believed he would give her this week—a baby.

"It's getting late. We need to head back," he said softly.

She heard his words. "I'm ready when you are," she said quietly, hoping she sounded more excited that she actually felt. In truth, she could stay here like this with him forever.

Forever.

She suddenly felt a shiver of apprehension slide down her spine. Why in the world would she think something like that? She'd never thought of forever when it came to any man and didn't intend to start now.

"You have beautiful breasts."

She watched his hand stroke her nipples as he spoke, using the same fingers he'd used to stroke between her legs earlier. His fingers were moist as he spread her very wetness over the hardened peaks of both breasts. Another shiver, this one of pleasure, ran up her spine. What on earth was he doing to her?

"Dominic…"

"Just close your eyes and feel, Taylor."

She did what he asked and the moment her eyelids fused shut she felt his tongue snaking out and capturing a bud, flickering over it, tasting her before closing in and taking it fully into his mouth. Desire, the kind she only knew with him, consumed her insides as she felt his mouth on her breasts, tasting, taunting and tampering with her in a way that was simply his. He feasted on one and then the other, almost sapping her of her senses, her sanity and her self-control.

And when his mouth found the indention of her belly and begin placing kisses all around it, she became lost within a maelstrom of sensations that had her surrendering to pleasure of the most erotic kind.

"You also have a beautiful stomach," he whispered with a warm breath before placing another kiss there. And then he whispered a few more French words and phrases and she wondered if he knew she understood what he was saying. She doubted it. Not that he was expressing his love or anything of the sort, but he was telling her in explicit French terms how much he loved making love to her body and just what being inside her did to him each and every time he was there. His words were making her succumb to emotions she was trying to control and didn't want to feel. They were also causing another deep hunger to take place inside her.

Then she felt the warmth of his breath move lower, and she held still, knowing what he was about to do. By now she should have grown accustomed to him kissing and caressing her there, but she wasn't. It couldn't be helped. He had a skill with his tongue whenever he went down on her that she just couldn't control, deny or resist. After all the lovemaking they'd shared that day she wondered how she would be able to handle this. She didn't know if she could take her body shattering in a million pieces again.

She opened her eyes to tell him but all she saw was his head, down between her legs and she could only close her eyes the moment his tongue flicked over her sensitive flesh.

Instinctively, her body came up off the bed and he grabbed her hips, holding her to his mouth as he devoured her with a sense of hunger that left her gasping for breath. She closed her eyes as sensations tore into her body once again.

She reached out for him, held his head in place, inviting him to go deeper, and he did, as his sinfully skilled and seductive tongue continued nonstop, increasing the pace, redefining the urgency. Her senses were being driven wild and her fingers threaded through his hair as he continued to ply long, deep, drugging kisses into her.

"Don't stop. Please don't stop," she cried out

over and over as a powerful throb overtook her. And then she felt it, some part of her that his tongue touched, that sent her over the edge, splintering her in two and making her scream yet again at the top of her lungs.

Slowly, deliberately, he continued to bestow the intimate kiss on her as she felt waves of heated pleasures float all through her, and she continued to writhe beneath his mouth.

She felt herself losing consciousness, and the last thing she remembered after moaning out his name was him pulling up and taking her mouth and she tasted herself on his tongue.

"What did you do to me?" Taylor asked moments after her lids fluttered back open. Dominic was leaning over her and wiping her brow with a warm, damp cloth.

He smiled down at her. "Do I truly need to answer that in full details, *chérie?*"

"No, but you did do something. I passed out for heaven's sake."

Yes, she had, he acknowledged silently. And just to think when they had left the resort earlier that day he had fully intended not to touch her. But whether he liked it or not, the woman made dreams a reality. She was the only woman he knew who could do something like that—and with very little effort.

"Tell me what you did, Dominic."

He heard the urgency in her voice. He'd known her long enough to realize she was someone who thrived on being in the know, especially when it concerned her personally.

"La petite mort," he said, using a French accent. "It's the French translation for *the little death* and a popular reference for a sexual orgasm. When pleasure gets so overwhelming it's considered a short period of transcendence one encounters."

"By passing out?"

"Yes."

He watched as she bit her bottom lip nervously before saying, "Nothing like that has ever happened to me before."

He was tempted to tell her nothing like that had ever happened to him, either. Although he hadn't passed out, he had felt pleasure so intense, even now parts of his body felt as if they were on fire. "It might happen again. But don't worry. You will be in good hands if it does," he assured her. He could tell from her expression that she intended to worry. Anxiety lines were forming around her lips. Her very beautiful, kissable lips. Lips that he was tempted to devour again.

Thinking he couldn't let that happen, he glanced at his watch. "Come on, it's time to get back."

He pushed the covers aside and stood and then reached a hand to help her up. He couldn't help staring at her naked body. The woman was so sinfully gorgeous, it was a shame.

"We'll take a shower when we get back," he said so she wouldn't be surprised when he pulled her into the shower with him later.

She only nodded as she got dressed. He finished before she did and glanced over at her to see her standing across from the mirror fussing with her hair. As he continued to watch her, he was amazed by the influx of emotions that consumed him, emotions he wasn't used to dealing with. Desire was something he understood. Lust was something he was used to, something he often craved. But he wasn't used to what he felt whenever he touched Taylor. And making love to her was another issue altogether.

She must have felt his eyes on her because she shifted her glance and met his gaze in the mirror. She smiled before twirling around for his inspection. "How do I look?"

He had to bite down to keep from saying, *"Like you belong to me."* Instead he said, "Beautiful as usual." He meant every word.

And then he crossed the room to her, needing to taste her one long, last time before he went up top to take his place at the wheel. Once they set sail he would have to concentrate on what he was doing and not on her. As if she knew his intent, exactly what was on his mind, she took the steps and met him halfway. And when he came to a stop in front of her, she reached up and placed her arms around his neck. He leaned down and connected his mouth to hers, angling his head for deeper penetration and releasing a satisfied groan when he got it.

Yes, this was the desire he understood, the lust he craved. But yet he couldn't discount that somewhere in the shadows lurked emotions he didn't want to cope with.

He didn't want to think about that now. He would find a way to deal with those unwanted emotions later.

"I had a nice time, Dominic," Taylor said as they entered their suite. The first thing she intended to do was take a shower and she couldn't help wondering if he would join her. She had never been a person who constantly had sex on her mind but around Dominic such a thing seemed as natural as breathing.

"I had a nice time, too," he said, tossing the room key on the table. "It's almost dinnertime. Do you have a particular taste for anything?"

She was glad his back was to her and he couldn't see her lick her lips. If only he knew what cravings had begun controlling her appetite recently. She shook her head, thinking that something was definitely wrong with her. She'd never been this hard up to get laid in her life and suddenly became suspicious of something. The resort had been the one to prepare the lunch they'd taken on board the ship, and she couldn't help wondering if perhaps some of the foods had contained some sort of the aphrodi-siac-laced ingredients that the brochure had bragged about using in a lot of their foods. After making love most of the afternoon, the idea of doing so again should be the furthest thing from her mind, but it wasn't.

"One of us got a call while we were out," Dominic said, claiming her attention as she watched him cross the room to the phone and its red blinking light.

She couldn't help wondering who could be call-ing. Her secretary knew not to bother her unless it was an extreme emergency and—

"It was for you," Dominic said, hanging the phone up. "A call from your sister Vanessa."

"Vanessa?" she said in surprise as she pulled her cell phone out of her pocket. She had turned it off earlier since she knew the reception on the ocean wouldn't be good. As she punched in Vanessa's number, she hoped everything was okay. Vanessa knew why she was there and would not have called unless it was important.

"Hello."

"Vanessa? It's Taylor. What's going on?"

"Taylor, I didn't want to bother you but Roz called."

Taylor lifted a brow. Roz Henry was Cheyenne's agent and good friend. "And?"

"And Cheyenne passed out during a photo shoot and was taken to the hospital."

Taylor frowned. Wanting to make sure she had

heard her sister correctly, she asked, "Cheyenne actually fainted?"

"Yes. Roz said she's okay but they are having a doctor check her out anyway."

Taylor knew how much her sister disliked doctors. "Where is Cheyenne?" she asked, knowing a photo shoot could take Cheyenne anywhere.

"She happens to be on one of those islands not far from where you are."

"Which one?"

A few minutes later Taylor was ending the call with her sister. She turned to find Dominic standing in the same spot he'd been standing when she had placed the call.

"Is there a problem?"

She glanced over at him and tried not to notice how sexy he looked standing there with his hands inside the pockets of his shorts. He had nice legs for a man. Muscular and bowed. "I don't know. Cheyenne passed out while doing a photo shoot. I need to make sure she's okay."

Dominic nodded and moved to stand in front of her. "Where is she?"

"On an island not far from here called Bimini Bay."

He appeared to consider her response for a mere second before saying, "Okay, then, let's go."

Taylor was amazed how quickly Dominic had made things happen. A half hour later a private plane had been chartered to take them to Bimini Bay. At twenty-three, Cheyenne was the youngest in the family and after a brief stint as a television reporter she'd tried her hand at modeling, saying it would give her the chance to travel and live in some of the most beautiful and exotic places. A few years ago she had purchased a home in Jamaica, but traveled back home for important family events, and like Taylor, she was on the board of the Steele Corporation.

Taylor couldn't help but smile when she thought of her sister, the rebel. She had taken being the baby in the Steele family to all-new heights. Her male cousins had thought Vanessa was a handful while growing up, but nothing had prepared them for Cheyenne. Whereas Vanessa and Taylor favored their father, Cheyenne had inherited their mother's strong Native American features, bestowing upon her an exotic look, which is why she was given the name of her mother's ancestry. She had beautiful brown skin, high cheekbones and dark eyes. Even as a child Cheyenne had gotten her share of admiring looks. It hadn't come as a surprise to anyone that while working as a news reporter a few years back, the president of a top modeling agency, who had seen her on television, had made Cheyenne an offer she couldn't refuse to come work for him.

"Here, drink this. It will calm your nerves."

She looked up as Dominic placed a cup of warm tea in her hand. From the moment she had told him of her concern for Cheyenne, he had seen to her every need. "Thank you," she said, taking the tea cup from him. She took a sip and liked the taste.

"We should be landing soon."

"Okay," she managed to say, not sure what Dominic was thinking. This was probably not the way he had envisioned their day ending. "Dominic, I know you must think it's silly that I'd want to see my sister just because she fainted and that—"

He placed a finger to her lips. "No, *chérie,* I don't think that at all. In fact I think it's rather sweet that you care for your sibling so much. But then I find that you are a very caring person."

He had given her the tea to calm her but she wondered if he knew the turbulence going through her at that moment being so close to him. In a way she felt she was out near the ocean, steadily getting pulled in by the tide. The man had that sort of effect. Even after what they had been doing that afternoon, she still wanted more of him. His heat was reaching out to her, warming her in one instant and sending shivers through her body in another.

"We'll make sure she's okay," he was saying. "And then we'll return to the resort later tonight."

"All right," she said, taking a sip.

His eyes seemed to have turned another shade of green, almost emerald. And there was a deep meaning in their dark depths. It was one she understood. He still wanted more of her, too. That thought sent more shivers through her and stirred her all the way down to her toes.

"Come here for a second," he said in a ragged breath. "Lean closer."

Placing the teacup aside, she leaned closer to him. When Dominic connected his mouth to hers, she thought that his kiss was like a drug. Highly potent. Very effective. It was electrifying every nerve in her body, uncoiling sensations she only felt when they were together.

"Buckle up, folks. We're about to land."

The pilot's voice intruded and she pulled away, reluctantly, from his hot and hungry mouth. "We will finish this later, right?" she couldn't help but ask, breathing the question against his moist lips.

"You can count on it, Taylor," was his quick response and she had no reason not to believe him.

Cheyenne Steele placed a faint smile on her face when she met Taylor's intense gaze. "I can't believe you came to check on me just because I fainted."

Taylor had found Cheyenne at the hotel where Roz had told her she was staying. After getting checked out by a doctor, Cheyenne had returned to her room to rest for the remainder of the day and had been surprised to open the door later that evening to find Taylor and a man she knew to be Dominic

Saxon. After Taylor had officially introduced them, he had left to wait downstairs in the lobby.

"Believe it," Taylor said, frowning. "You just better be glad Vanessa and I decided not to mention anything about it to Mama. I noticed you didn't look well when we were home a few weeks ago and have been concerned about it ever since. I figured you're working crazy hours and not taking proper care of yourself. So tell me what the doctor said. Am I right? Are you not eating enough for that vigorous schedule you're keeping? Starving yourself to keep your weight down?"

Cheyenne waved off her words. "I'm fine. Just got a little overheated. Now enough about me. Tell me how things are going with you and Dominic."

Taylor knew Cheyenne was trying to shift the focus off her and onto Dominic, but she refused to let her. For some reason Taylor didn't believe Cheyenne's story about heat exhaustion, although with the island's hot temperature, getting over-heated was a possibility. Taylor had a feeling that there was something else, something Cheyenne wasn't telling her. She could feel it. And for one thing, Cheyenne was looking everywhere but at her.

"Forget about me and Dominic. What's going on, Chey?" she asked softly "You're lying to me and I don't like it. Are you on an anorexia kick or something? I know how crazy you get sometimes about keeping your model figure and how you—"

"No, that's not it," Cheyenne said quickly.

Taylor breathed in deeply. "Then what is it? What aren't you telling me?"

The silence that suddenly descended upon the room was unnerving. And just when she thought Cheyenne would not say anything, her sister opened her mouth and spoke. "Okay, I'll tell you, but you must promise not to tell anyone. Not Van or the cousins and especially not Mama. I'll tell everyone when I come home for Marcus's high school graduation in a few weeks."

Taylor's brows drew together in a frown. "Tell them what?"

"You have to promise."

Taylor rolled her eyes. "Okay, okay, I promise. So what are you going to tell them?"

Cheyenne's eyes, a color so dark they looked black, stared straight into hers when she said, "That I'm pregnant."

"Are you all right, Taylor?"

Taylor glanced up at Dominic. "Yes, I'm okay."

The plane had landed and they had returned to the resort. After getting over the initial shock of what Cheyenne had told her, she had talked her sister into going out to dinner with her and Dominic at one of the restaurants near the hotel. The three of them had had a nice time and she could tell that Cheyenne liked Dominic. When it came to men

Cheyenne could be downright nitpicky, which made
Taylor wonder about the identity of the man who
had fathered Cheyenne's baby. He'd certainly had
to have been someone Cheyenne had been quite
taken with. When she'd asked Cheyenne about the
man, she had refused to talk about him, only saying
that he was someone she had met once and would
probably never see again.

"Are you still worried about your sister? She
seems to be doing okay now," Dominic said, breaking into her thoughts.

If only you knew, she thought. Of course she
hadn't mentioned anything to Dominic about her
sister's condition, and didn't want to think what the
family would have to say when Cheyenne dropped
her little bombshell. Although Taylor had made
plans to do the baby thing solo, her family wouldn't
have been surprised if she was to pop up pregnant
without the benefit of a husband because they all
knew how much Taylor loved children, and with her
methodical mind, having a child without a husband
would seem like something Taylor would do.

But Cheyenne was another matter altogether.
Besides being the baby in the family who got all the
attention, Cheyenne was never a person to fawn
over babies and had never mentioned that she
wanted any of her own. Her modeling career was
the only thing she really cared about and the thought
of gaining weight was simply a no-no.

But when Taylor had inquired if she was contemplating getting an abortion, Cheyenne had surprised her by saying under no circumstances would she consider such a thing. That made Taylor proud of her baby sister's desire to accept full responsibility for her actions and accept whatever sacrifices that had to be made.

Once again, Taylor's thoughts shifted to the man who had gotten Cheyenne to lower her guard. Cheyenne was one to get annoyed with men easily, especially those who got stuck on her features. She said she would never know if the man loved her for herself or her looks. Since she had been oohed and aahed over most of her life, to Cheyenne a man loving her for herself and not her beauty was important. Although Taylor wasn't sure about the mystery man's feelings, she knew her sister well enough to know that during their brief encounter, Cheyenne must have fallen in love with him.

"Taylor?"

She then realized she hadn't answered Dominic's question. "I worry about Cheyenne out of habit," she said. "Vanessa and I both do, although Cheyenne has shown us time and time again that she's quite capable of taking care of herself. She's traveled more places than I ever have or probably ever will, and lives in Jamaica, a long way from home. I'm also her wealth and asset manager so I know that she's doing very well financially."

"But?"

Taylor chuckled. "How do you know there's a *but* in there?"

He smiled down at her as they stepped onto the elevator that would take them up to their suite. "Because I'm beginning to know you, Taylor. With you, some things are easy to figure out."

She wondered at that. Had he figured out how much she wanted him? Or even worse, had he figured out that she had fallen head over heels in love with him? She had been bordering on the edge since the first time they had made love, but had gotten a pretty big shove when he had seen how much she'd been worried about Cheyenne and had chartered a plane and whisked her to the island where her sister was, to calm her fears. She didn't know too many men who would have done that. Most would have been annoyed that she was letting worrying about her sister infringe upon their time with her.

"You're right, there is a *but*. However, the last thing I plan on doing is getting into Cheyenne's business. I let my sisters deal with their own issues, but they know I'm there if they need me."

Dominic nodded. "You must be exhausted. When we get up to the room, I'll run bathwater for you. A good hot soak will do you good."

She turned toward him and placed her arms around his neck, glad they were the only people in the elevator. "Um, that sounds nice, but what about you?"

He smiled and that full smile on such a pair of sensual lips that showed beautiful white teeth started a slow, aching throb in her center. "I'll take a shower later."

She shook her head. "We agreed that the next time you got in the shower I would be there with you."

He chuckled. "Yes, but you're too tired tonight and I understand."

She knew he did understand, and that's what made him so beautiful in her eyes. He had such an understanding spirit when it came to her. "But I'm not too tired for that, Dominic," she said softly.

What she didn't add was that she needed him tonight in a way she had never needed him before. Now that she knew that she loved him, she wanted not only his seed to get her pregnant, nor just his body that always gave her pleasure. What she wanted more than anything was everything that was him. They had only five days left and she wanted to spend each and every moment intimately with him.

"Are you sure?" he asked, staring down at her. His eyes had changed to a soft green and were looking straight into hers.

"I'm positive." When it came to him, there was no way she could or ever would be not sure of anything. He was the first man she could admit to loving and probably would be the only man she would ever love. It was just her luck that the one man who had finally captured her heart would be someone who was dead set against ever marrying again, a man intent on not allowing his heart to ever belong to another woman. A man who was still in love with his dead wife.

"Why are you frowning, *chérie?*"

His gaze burned into hers with an intensity that seared her skin, made her want him just that much more. "No reason, other than I need to make sure it's what you want, too," she decided to say. "After all we've done today, are you sure you're not too tired? If you are, then I can certainly understand."

She suddenly found herself whisked off her feet into strong arms and when he leaned down and kissed her, he practically drew the breath from her lungs. The scent of him surrounded her, practically oozed from wall to wall, panel to panel, in the elevator. It was warm, musky with a whiff of the sea that still clung to him, as well.

Only when he withdrew his mouth from hers, leaving the taste of him on her tongue, did she allow herself to breathe. And only when the elevator door swooshed open to their floor, and he stepped out, still carrying her in his arms, did she speak, barely breathing his name against his neck.

"Dominic…"

When they stopped in front of their door and he shifted her in his arms to pull out his passkey she realized that something hot, heavy and passionate was taking place between them, had been taking place since they had arrived on the island. Shivers of anticipation raced down her spine, sensitized every nerve and sent an uncontrollable urge to her brain, making awareness flow rapidly through her body.

When he opened the door, placed her on her feet before closing and locking it behind them, she released a long, ragged breath. It was past midnight already, but time was not a factor here; it could never be a factor between them. The only thing that mattered was that she was about to make love yet again to the man she loved.

He leaned back against the door and stared at her and she felt it like an intimate caress. She may not have his love but she definitely had his desire. And it was a potent thing, like a stimulating drug that actually had hot blood flowing through her veins, making her head spin, logical thoughts disintegrating and making the throb between her legs become an ache that he needed to take care of.

Only him.

Without thinking about what she was doing and knowing that he was watching her every move, she began undressing as she slowly walked backward toward the bedroom. First came her top and she tossed it aside. She paused long enough to kick away her sandals before continuing her trek backward. By the time she reached the bedroom door her clothes laid a trail on the floor and only her panties remained.

He stood there, still leaning against the door, not having moved an inch. But something on him had definitely grown…not that it hadn't been big before. She had felt it when he had picked her up in his arms and again when he had slid her body down his when he had placed her on her feet. But now as her gaze zeroed in on the crotch of his shorts, she saw him enlarging before her eyes just the way she wanted. And just the way she needed.

"Dominic…" She breathed out his name on a sigh, and that's when he moved, slowly walking toward her, pausing to undress, as well. By the time he reached her in the bedroom doorway, he was totally and completely naked.

It was then that she watched as he got down on his knees to remove the final piece of clothing from her body—for the second time that day—a pair of skimpy black lace panties. But he didn't stop there once he had removed them and had tossed them aside.

Dominic felt the need for Taylor all the way to the bone. He knew her scent, and after spending an afternoon making love to her on the boat, his tongue was practically drenched with her taste. He leaned forward and rested his face against the warm skin of her thigh and inhaled the essence of her femininity, so close to his face.

He felt the hands she had placed on his shoulders

as if she was depending on his strength to hold her up. In his position, kneeling on the floor in front of her, he was just where he wanted to be, up close and as personal as he could get.

Not really.

There was this one thing that immediately demanded his attention, something his tongue was throbbing to do, something he hadn't gotten enough of doing earlier that day. He shifted his head and found the spot he wanted, gripped her hips and letting his tongue go to work, tasting her with a hunger that he knew she had to feel. He pushed her legs apart even farther so he could delve deeper, his tongue could penetrate farther, taking on a life of its own inside her.

He heard her moans, gloried in her groans. Felt the way her fingers were digging hard into his shoulders, the way she was arching the lower part of her body to lock in on his mouth. His heart rate began racing. His thirst for her taste was unquenchable. The more he got, the more he wanted, and he was letting her know it, feel it. There was just something about kissing her this way that made everything inside him react, summoned all his inner resources.

Moments later he felt her body jerk beneath his mouth and heard her scream, but he ignored the sound and kept doing what he was doing. He had the ability to climax just from tasting her, and was fighting like hell not to do so. He wanted to take her in the shower, while the force of the water beat down on them. At that point when it happened, he wanted something else other than his tongue inside her. He wanted to explode inside her, to give her the very thing that would give her his baby, if he hadn't already done so.

Dominic pulled back, quickly stood and scooped her up into his arms. He felt her go limp and knew if the water didn't revive her, something else definitely would. He stepped into the shower and quickly turned on the water. A soon as the water was warm he stepped under it and eased Taylor out of his arms to stand in front of him and then brought her close to him as he lifted her off her feet.

"Wrap your legs around me, *chérie*," he said in a deep, husky voice.

She did what he asked and before her mind could register what he was about to do, he swiftly entered her. Water poured down on them, blurring their vision, soaking their hair, but nothing could stop him from backing her up against the tile wall and pumping in and out of her like a man pushed over the edge. A man who wanted to die remembering how it was to be inside her this way.

And just in case those other times they had made love didn't quite do the trick, he grabbed hold of the hips that cradled his pelvis, drove deeper into her the exact moment he felt his entire body explode, forcing himself to hold still while feeling her muscles clench everything out of him, and he still kept coming, filling her to capacity in a way he had never done any other woman.

He showed no sign of even thinking about releasing her after becoming fully spent, totally drained. Like before, he wanted his body to remain connected to hers so he adjusted his stance, braced his legs apart and kept her pinned to the wall.

While the water was still cascading down on them, he lifted his head and met her gaze. The look in her eyes did something to him. There had been a sudden flash of something that had passed through the dark gaze holding his. He was certain of it. But what?

Dominic refused to take time to figure anything out. Not now and not here. He felt his body getting hard inside her all over again. He reached up and turned off the water before opening the shower door. And with her still in his arms, her body intimately joined to his, he stepped out of the shower.

With warm water still soaking their skin he managed to grab a big, thick towel off the rack and wrap it around them before leaving the bathroom. He reached the bed and then tumbled onto the snow-white bedcovers with her in his arms. And then he straddled her body and stared down at her, not understanding the sudden obsession and possession he felt. It was more than the fact that she could even now be carrying his child, a Saxon heir. Nor was it about the way his body was able to respond to hers, and kept responding in ways it had never done to other women. But it did have something to do with the warm prickling sensation that was running over his damp skin and the fire that was flowing in his blood. And for one pulse-stopping moment he felt as if he was going through an addiction. One part of his mind was telling him that the one thing he needed to do before getting in deeper was to pull back and take the stance that if she hadn't gotten pregnant by now, then too bad. He couldn't run the risk of letting her get under his skin, wiggle her way anywhere near his heart.

But he couldn't summon the strength to do that or think that way. At the moment he was just where he wanted to be: inside her while her muscles clenched him tight, milked him for all she could get. She had a strong hold on him as he had a strong hold on her and it seemed neither of them was going anywhere or wanted to handle whatever was happening right now any differently.

So he began doing what he enjoyed doing— moving inside her, thrusting in and out of her with long, leisurely, slow strokes, while watching her facial expression with each stimulating massage. Just as she was watching his. He was certain that his need, this unexplainable, overwhelming desire, was there, clearly visible on his face for her to see, as hers was fully exposed to him. Like all the other times before, he was putting everything into this mating, all of himself, everything that was in him he was giving to her. Freely and unselfishly. For her it seemed he could do nothing less.

And then he leaned closer to her mouth, needing the taste of her. And when his tongue began mating with hers in that same tempo their bodies were mating, something hot and urgent flared through him, uncoiled within his stomach and he increased the rhythm and began pumping madly, with a raw, primal need that had him locked in its grip. In the deep recesses of his mind he heard her scream out his name, automatically triggering something inside him and his body bucked hard at the same time that he screamed out hers.

And then it happened again, as it always did with her. He felt a scorching sensation throughout his body, shivers passing through every nerve, as he shot an abundance of life-creating fluid inside her while breathing in her scent, their scent. And he knew that if he lived to be over a hundred, he would never get tired of making love to Taylor Steele.

And as he leaned forward and cradled his face in the crook of her neck, he decided that to think such a thing was simply too disturbing to dissect at the moment.

Chapter 9

Taylor stood at the window and looked out at the beauty of the island and the way the ocean seemed to come to peace when the waves hit the shoreline. For the rest of her life she would always remember this place. It held so many memories. Memories she would cherish forever.

It seemed so unfair that the week had come and gone so quickly and it was time for her and Dominic to leave with hope that together they had created a life, a life they would ultimately share over the years. In the beginning the thought of them doing so wasn't a problem. That was when she was only interested in a baby and not a relationship...and certainly not love.

Love.

There was no doubt in her mind that she loved Dominic with every sense of her being. It was love not lust. She hadn't gotten the two confused as she had tried convincing herself a number of times over the past few days. She loved him in bed or out, although she had to admit they had spent more time during the past week in bed.

Because they were so sure she had conceived, they had talked about names for their child and had decided if it was a boy they would name him Amaury and for a girl, she wanted Dominique. From the look that had appeared on his face when she had made her request, she could tell he had been touched that she wanted to name their daughter after him. And then he had asked something of her that was unexpected. He wanted to be there when she found out if she had gotten pregnant and asked if she would let him. She had agreed that he could and was touched that he even wanted to be.

Suddenly, her senses went on full alert. He hadn't made a sound but she knew the exact moment he had entered the room. She could actually feel his body heat getting closer as he crossed the room toward her. And then he was standing directly behind her. She could feel the warmth of his breath coming into contact with her neck. Instinctively, she leaned back at the same moment he wrapped strong arms around her waist, holding her tight. Her bottom was cradled snug against his center and she immediately felt the huge bulge she had gotten used to.

"See what you do to me every time," he whispered in her ear. "It's totally insane for me to want you so much."

"Mmm" was the only thing she could manage to murmur as she closed her eyes, knowing memories like this would have to sustain her forever. In a short while they would be leaving to return to America—and their lives apart. She would return to her world and he would return to his. Their week-long visit to the island, their procreation vacation, would be something of the past, something they hoped, they truly believed would show results.

She refused to open her eyes when she felt his lips at the base of neck, then moving slightly to taste the area beneath her ear in one warm lick. Shivers ran through her body. He was making her want him and he knew it. "How much time do we have?" she asked, without opening her eyes. Instead she leaned back farther and angled her head in such a way that his lips could explore her more. Now he was kissing her cheek, the fine line of her jaw.

"As much time as we want. Martin has arrived with the plane but we fly out when I say we do."

She opened her eyes knowing just what that meant. They wanted each other again. Hadn't gotten enough. And before leaving they would make time.

She slowly turned in his arms and their gazes

met. No further words were needed. There was nothing left to be said. After today there would be no reason for them to come together like this.

But today. For now. There was a reason. One that was old as time and as primal as mankind. And they would share it…one last time.

He began taking slow steps backward and she followed, not that she had a choice, with his arms still around her waist. She thought of all the things they had shared, all those different positions they had tried and those others he had thrown in—had introduced her to—for good measure. Over the past seven days she had definitely become sexually educated. Had graduated a star pupil.

Now she intended to put that education to work.

"I want to taste you all over, Dominic," she whispered, just inches from his lips. "And then I plan to ride you until you say you've had enough."

"I'll never say it's enough," he murmured back hotly, taking his tongue and flicking it out to moisten her lips.

"We'll see." And then she pushed him back on the bed and began going after him with a hunger and urgency that surprised even her. She pulled off his clothes, actually sent buttons flying in her haste and then she shifted to remove her own clothing. When they were both naked she went after his mouth, pressing hers to his, sinking her fingers into his scalp.

Three hours later when exhaustion finally claimed

the two of them, he admitted it was all he could handle in one day, but had been quick to say it still wasn't enough.

"So, do you think you're pregnant?"

Taylor pondered Vanessa's question before opening her mouth to speak. Then without saying anything she closed it. Vanessa, who was sitting across the table from her, lifted a brow. "Well?"

The two had made plans to meet for lunch when Vanessa had called earlier in the week to say she would be flying to D.C. to attend a three-day seminar hosted by the Public Relations Society of America.

Taylor smiled. Vanessa had a way of getting any information out of you by doing something called "digging in." It was better to go ahead and give her an answer without subjecting yourself to such torture. "Yes, I know I'm pregnant."

Vanessa blinked. She knew that Taylor hadn't been back from her island rendezvous a full week yet. "You skipped a period already?"

"No, not yet, but I don't need that to confirm what I already know." She didn't add that Dominic had been too thorough for her not to be pregnant.

Dominic.

Had it been only five days since she had seen him last? Five days since he had kissed her when he had dropped her off at the Reagan National Airport before continuing his flight to Los Angeles to visit his parents? Five long miserable days where her body seemed to be going through some form of sexual withdrawal when she would wake up during the night to reach for him and he wasn't there?

Vanessa slanted her a look. "For you to be so sure of something like that means Dominic Saxon is one hell of a potent individual or that he was pretty good at what you wanted him to do."

Taylor could only smile again. "Both. Enough about me and Dominic. How are things going with the wedding?"

For the next thirty or so minutes over lunch she listened while her sister told her how the wedding plans were coming and how Vanessa's best friend, Sienna, had been hired to remodel Cameron's home in Charlotte, the house where the couple would be living. Because Cameron's business took him just about anywhere in the world, he had homes in other places, as well, including a beautiful one next door to Cheyenne's in Jamaica.

"And you are coming home to Marcus's high school graduation in a couple of weeks, aren't you?" Vanessa interrupted her thoughts by asking.

"I wouldn't miss it." What she wouldn't say, because of the promise she had made to Cheyenne, was that Vanessa would find out in two weeks that she would be an aunt twice over. It was a definite that Cheyenne was pregnant, and by that time Taylor would know if she was pregnant, as well.

* * *

A week later Dominic still found that he was in that same melancholy mood. He walked through his home thinking how he had turned down several dinner invitations from friends. A woman who was someone he would often sleep with when he got the urge had called—several times—blatantly inviting him to spend the night with her and he had turned her down, as well. He knew Ivy was pretty pissed at the thought that he had ignored her not once but twice, but he hadn't cared enough to even send her flowers to smooth things over.

The only woman he could think about, the only woman he wanted was Taylor. He was convinced that during the week they had spent together, he had gotten bewitched by her beauty or her ability to please him in bed. He was totally taken by the entire package, which included those things and a lot more. Without even trying, she had left a mark on him that no other woman could wipe away.

And he didn't like the thought of that one damn bit.

He was a single man, and one with a strong sexual appetite. So why was he denying himself the company of beautiful women, women who would want more from him than just a baby? But he knew the answer to that one.

There was no woman who had the ability to literally charge the air between them the moment she walked into a room other than Taylor Steele. No other woman who could bring him almost to his knees with just one kiss—a kiss he had taught her how to perfect. And then there were the times he would be inside her…

Just thinking about it made his entire body ache for something he couldn't have but desperately wanted. When he reached the kitchen he pulled open the refrigerator and decided he needed a cold glass of water. He'd been dreaming again about Taylor, about them making love. The dream had seemed so real he had awakened in a heated sweat.

"Hey, are you okay?"

Dominic glanced over his shoulder at Ryder. "Yeah, I'm fine. Why aren't you in bed?"

"I just got in from the gym."

Dominic glanced at the clock on the kitchen wall. "This late?"

"Yes. This late."

He watched the huge hulk of a man slide into a chair at the kitchen table. Not for the first time he wondered about Ryder, the man who had been his bodyguard, his confidant and friend for close to twenty years now. Ryder never mentioned a family, although Dominic knew there was some special woman back in France and he left to return there every chance he got. At least Dominic figured it was a woman since whenever Ryder came back he had a better disposition. More than once over the years he'd tried inquiring about Ryder's other life and if it included a family, but the man had effectively and intentionally changed the subject, letting Dominic know any discussion about him was off-limits.

"So, how did you enjoy your week on Latois?"

Dominic glanced over at Ryder. He hadn't told anyone where he would be that week other than Matt and he was certain Matt hadn't mentioned anything to anyone. His secretary had been informed that if an emergency came up to contact Matt. So where had Ryder gotten his information?

"Don't bother figuring things out, Nick. I know where you are 24-7. It's my business to protect you. It's what your grandfather sent me here to do."

Dominic closed the refrigerator and leaned back against it. He felt irritated that his grandfather intended to be a part of his life even when he didn't want him to. "It's been close to twenty years now, Ryder?" he asked angrily. "You can't be my bodyguard forever. Besides, I don't need one anymore." Even though he said the words he knew over the years Ryder had become more than just his bodyguard.

"You are who you are. You will always need someone to watch your back."

"My grandfather's orders?" Dominic asked angrily.

"When are you going to stop hating him?"

Dominic sighed. He and Ryder had had this conversation several times. For some reason Ryder was very loyal to Franco Saxon.

"I don't hate him actually," Dominic said calmly.

"I just don't want him to be a part of my life just like he chose not to be a part of my father's life when he married my mother."

"He made a mistake Nick. Your father has forgiven him. So has your mother."

"I'm glad to hear it. Now I'm going back to bed." Dominic turned to leave but Ryder's next question stopped him.

"And what of the new Saxon heir?"

Dominic slowly turned around and stared at Ryder. Did he have no secrets from this man? He wouldn't waste his time trying to figure out how Ryder had known he was on Latois for the sole purpose of making a baby. It would have been simple enough since the island advertised heavily their procreation vacations.

"You tell me. What about the new Saxon heir?"

"Your parents and your grandfather would be pleased that you're carrying the family line forward."

Dominic was glad his parents would be overjoyed with the news, but as for his grandfather, he really didn't give a royal damn. "Nothing is definite yet."

Ryder chuckled at that. "But I'm sure it will be. You're a Saxon."

Dominic arched a brow. "Meaning?"

"You'll make it happen."

Dominic walked out of the room thinking he certainly hoped so. But he would continue to be on pins and needles while he waited for Taylor's call.

* * *

It was time to call Dominic.

Taylor placed the package she has purchased at the drugstore on the table. There was no reason why she couldn't just march into the bathroom and find out now and just call and give Dominic the results. Yes, there was a reason. He had asked to be present when she found out and she had promised him that he could. She would keep her promise.

It had been twelve days and five hours since she had seen Dominic last, but there had not been one single day that she had not gone to bed thinking of him or awakened with him in her thoughts, as well. And then there were those moments during the day when out of nowhere she would remember something—a look he'd given her, a touch. And heaven help her when she would recall all the times they made love, all those different positions…

Shivers of awareness ran down her spine. She didn't need a pregnancy test to tell her what she knew in her heart was already true. She was pregnant with Dominic's child. There was no way that she couldn't be.

Now she needed to place that call.

She walked over to the sofa and sat down then reached for the telephone and punched his private number.

"Hello, Taylor."

Immediately, upon hearing his strong, husky

voice, an electric current seemed to have run right through her. She swallowed and then asked, "How did you know it was me?"

"Caller ID."

She nodded. That made sense. "You wanted me to call you when it was time."

"And is it time to find out?" he asked.

"Yes."

"I'm on my way over."

He'd said it as though he was right up the street. "Will you be arriving tomorrow?"

"No, I'm on my way to your place now. I've been in D.C. staying at the Saxon Hotel for the last two days. I wanted to be close by when you called and figured it would be soon," he informed her.

"Oh."

"I'll see you in less than an hour, Taylor."

"Okay."

And then he ended the call.

Chapter 10

Taylor glanced at herself in the mirror one final time after hearing the sound of the doorbell. A surge of anxiety swept through her. How was she supposed to act when she saw Dominic again? He wasn't just any man, but was someone she had spent an entire week making love with more than eighty percent of the time. The last four days on Latois had been the most intense. It was as if they were counting down the hours, minutes and seconds and wanted to make each one count.

She glanced down at her outfit, a pair of shorts and a tank top. She had wanted to appear casual, right at home and had taken a shower and put on a little makeup and sprayed on her favorite cologne.

She crossed the room and inhaled deeply, hoping and praying she would be able to keep things together when she saw him. She opened the door and whatever words of greeting she planned to say died on her lips. All she could do was stand there and stare at him.

For a few split seconds it seemed neither of them was capable of speaking, since he was staring back at her. Then, he finally spoke in a deep, raspy voice that sent shivers all through Taylor's body.

"It's good seeing you again, Taylor."

She inhaled deeply once more. "It's good seeing you again, as well, Dominic." She had to admit that she sounded slightly hoarse to her own ears. "Won't you come in?"

She took a step back and he entered, closing the door behind him. He glanced around a second before returning his gaze to her. "You look good."

"Thanks, and so do you." And she meant it. He was wearing a dark gray suit and white shirt and looked gorgeous as ever. "Would you like something to drink?"

"What do you have?"

"Whatever you want." Too late she realized how that may have sounded.

He chuckled softly. "In that case, a glass of wine would be nice."

"No problem. Make yourself comfortable and I'll be right back." She headed toward the kitchen but couldn't help glancing over her shoulder and saw that he was removing his jacket, exposing those broad shoulders she remembered so well.

A tingling sensation flowed through her as she recalled a number of other things, and they were things she wished she wouldn't remember right now. Her body was heated enough already.

Once she got to the kitchen she let out a deep breath. The sexual chemistry they'd shared hadn't been just confined to the island. It was here in her apartment. She'd felt it the moment she opened the door and saw him standing there. There was no way he hadn't felt it, too.

With nervous hands she poured him a glass of wine and poured a glass of apple juice for herself. "I can do this," she murmured softly before leaving her kitchen.

He was standing by the window, looking at the beautiful view of the Potomac and turned when he heard her enter the room. His gaze met hers and she actually saw the heated lust in his eyes. Suddenly, she felt hotter than before and could actually feel dampness form on her forehead. With all the strength she could muster, she made it across the room to him without dropping the glasses out of her hand.

"Here you are. I hope I wasn't too long."

He smiled before taking the glass from her trembling hand. "No, you weren't."

Their fingers touched and she felt a sizzling sensation all the way to her toes. All she had to do was reconnect with his gaze to know he'd felt it, as well. Thinking the cold apple juice would certainly cool her off, she quickly took a sip. It didn't do any good. Heat was still trickling through her.

"So how have you been feeling?" he asked, breaking into the silence that had surrounded them.

"I've been fine. Busy as usual. I had a lot to catch up on when I got back."

"So did I."

"The stock market has looked good for the past couple of weeks," she said, leading him over to the sofa to sit down. He sat on one end and she on the other.

"Yes, I saw that."

The room plunged back into silence and she began racking her brain for something else to say. She thought about a recent news article and brought it up. He made a comment or two and that was it. Deciding she was dragging things out for no reason at all she said, "I'm sure you have a lot to do this evening, so if you want we can find out if I'm pregnant or not right now."

"I don't have anything to do this evening," he said smoothly. "Do you feel pregnant?"

A smile touched her lips. "If you're asking if I've had morning sickness or anything like that, then the answer is no. I feel wonderful. But I have missed my period by a few days."

"Oh."

Too late she wondered if she had said too much, then decided no, she hadn't. While on the island they had talked about a number of things, personal things regarding changes that would take place to her body once she became pregnant. She had felt comfortable discussing them with him then and there was no reason she shouldn't feel at ease talking about them with him now. Although most of the time they had held the discussions while both of them had been wrapped in each other's arms, naked and satiated after having just made love.

"What about your breasts?"

Desire sparked in the center of her, right below the waist, between the legs. "What about them?" she asked softly.

He took a sip of wine before leaning forward. "Are they tender? You said that would be one sure-tell sign."

Yes, she had said that. "Ah, yes. They are somewhat tender."

"I see."

He was staring at her, more specifically her breasts. They had definitely become the subject of his intense assessment. A part of her wanted to take her hands and cover them, not that he could see anything through her blouse. But then she felt her nipples harden and didn't have to glance down at herself to know that he probably saw how the tips were pressed against her blouse.

She quickly got to her feet, feeling somewhat shaky and still feeling hot. "I-I'll go in and do the test now."

He got to his feet, as well. "There's no hurry, Taylor. I'm enjoying your company. Come on, let's sit back down."

He reached out and touched her arm and they both discovered within seconds it had been a mistake. Suddenly, it was as if the two weeks' separation hadn't happened and they were back on the island, in their suite, where getting naked and making love had become as normal to them as breathing.

Her heart began racing when she saw him lower his head toward hers and she knew what she was in for. However, she also knew what she couldn't have. She loved him but he didn't love her and she refused to be one of those women who pined away for a love that would never be.

With all the strength she could muster, she pulled her hand from within his grasp and took a step back. "I—I think I need to go and do that test now," she said with a quiver in her voice as she steadily backed away from him.

His eyes bored into hers. She could still feel the sensuous heat. "Need help?" he asked in a voice that sent more shivers up her spine.

"No, thanks. I can handle things." And then she turned and quickly rushed off toward the bathroom.

Dominic placed his hands in the pockets of his slacks as he walked back over to the window. He hadn't meant to make Taylor feel uncomfortable, but seeing her again had done something to him. The moment she had opened the door he had wanted to reach out and sweep her off her feet and kiss her with all the intensity that he felt. He had firsthand knowledge of just how wonderful she would feel in his arms and just how delicious her taste was. He had missed both over the past two weeks.

He'd had to constantly force himself to accept that he couldn't call her and she wouldn't be calling him. What had been between them was nothing more than a business agreement. He wasn't supposed to start having these intense emotions. Nor was he supposed to think of her during every waking moment, remembering what they had shared on that island.

But the fact of the matter was that he couldn't forget. Neither his mind nor his body would let him. He would wake up during the middle of the night actually inhaling her scent. It was during those times when his senses would get stirred to a degree that he thought he was losing his mind. Never in his life had any woman affected him so deeply, made him want her so badly.

The sound of footsteps had him turning around

and his gaze immediately latched onto her face when she came back into the room. His heartbeat kicked hard in his chest when he saw the tears that glistened in her eyes. Were they tears of joy or of disappointment? What if she hadn't gotten pregnant as he had so arrogantly assumed?

Somehow he made his body move and crossed the room to her. Automatically he reached out and wiped one of her tears away with the tip of his finger. When she didn't say anything for the longest time, just stood gazing at him, he asked in a near-quiet tone, "Are you or aren't you?"

As he watched her face, he saw a smile touch the corners of her lips. Then she nodded. "Yes, I am. Oh, Dominic, we're having a baby," she said in such an awed voice that to him it was like a match thrown in a box of bone-dry tinder. The blaze within him had flared into a full flame.

He was going to be a father.

The realization of that hit him and he hadn't known just how much he'd wanted that until now. He could no more stop himself from kissing her at that moment than he could stop the day from turning into night. He reached out and pulled her into his arms and in one smooth sweep, captured her lips as if doing so was the most natural thing.

There was something in knowing the man whose hot and hungry mouth was insistently eating away at hers, was the man whose child she carried in her womb. Coupled with the fact that she loved him with all her heart she forgot that the last thing they should be doing was sharing a kiss.

Neither should they be tearing away at each other's clothes, but they were doing that, too. She hadn't forgotten what this was like. An intense desire to mate. Nor had she forgotten the feel of wanting him with such a raw, primitive need like what she was feeling now.

One part of her mind was saying this was crazy, totally insane. They weren't thinking rationally. All she had to say to that was, yes, probably not. But at that precise moment she was happier than any one woman had a right to be. She was having a baby. A baby that she had created with the man she loved. She would have plenty of time tomorrow to be reminded that he didn't love her. Right now he desired her and that was enough.

He broke off the kiss, mainly to give them a chance to breathe. And then he pulled her back into his arms to finish removing her clothes. But in her opinion that wasn't going fast enough. "Hurry, Dominic."

Once he had her completely naked, he began removing his own clothes at a fast pace. She wasn't helping matters when each time he exposed a portion of naked skin, her mouth and lips were there, wanting to taste him all over, practically everywhere.

It seemed at that moment he made the correct assumption they would never make it to the bedroom and pulled her down with him to the carpeted floor. He then shifted his body for her to straddle his.

She stared down at him. "You know since I'm already pregnant there's no earthly reason for us to be doing this," she said in a rushed and fevered voice.

"Is there an unearthly one?" he asked in a voice so hoarse she could barely hear him.

"None that I can think of."

"Good. Do you want me to stop?" he asked and then leaned up his head to give the hardened tip of her breast one tantalizing lick.

"Ah, no. Don't stop. Whatever you do, *please* don't stop."

"I won't," he muttered against her other breast and flicked a lick to it before pulling and giving it a tug with his lips.

She threw her head back and let out a deep moan. It was shameless. It brought to life every sensual part of her. And when she felt the hard, moist tip of his erection, right there at the entrance of her feminine core, she only knew but one way to go. Down.

She pressed her weight down on him and the hands he'd used earlier to wipe away her tears held her hips in a tight grip. And when she felt him inside her, all the way to the hilt, she knew what she had to do. What she wanted to do.

Ride him.

And since he seemed amenable to letting her be in control, she took it. She slowly eased up, just an inch or so short of their bodies disconnecting and then she eased back down, then up again, repeating the process as she slid up and down on him, over and over again, hearing his sharp indrawn breath every time her hips shifted back and forth over him.

"Taylor…"

She didn't want to focus on the tortured way he was saying her name. Instead she stared down at the expressions on his face. The look was intoxicating her senses, practically blowing her mind. The slow, steady heat between her legs where their bodies connected suddenly seemed filled with an electrical charge that sent shock waves frolicking through her body.

She arched her back and released an intense scream. Dominic quickly pulled her mouth down to his and kissed her with a hunger that splintered her body in a million pieces. And then she felt him explode inside her while his hands kept a tight grip on her hips.

She became lost in sensations she had been certain she would never feel again. But she was feeling them now, thanks to Dominic. What they were sharing was perfect, so unerringly flawless, it was as if they were the only two living souls in the entire universe. It was as if she couldn't get enough of him and he couldn't get enough of her.

And as she clung to his shoulders as yet another orgasm struck her, she couldn't help but wonder just where would they go from here?

"You've bewitched me, Taylor."

They had moved from the living room floor to the bedroom an hour or so ago. Taylor lay beside Dominic but didn't turn her head to look at him. The truth of the matter was that she didn't have the strength to move even if she wanted to. Instead she reached out and touched his erection that hadn't gone down. "And I could give you a list of all the things you've done to me, Dominic."

She then reached out and brought his hand to her stomach. "But putting your baby in here, I think, is the most precious of them all."

Her words must have touched him because he shifted his body and lowered his lips to hers. Like all the others, this kiss was hot, sexual and sent a flaming sensation all through her. Moments later, to her disappointment he pulled back and met her gaze.

"I want to take you out to dinner to celebrate."

"Tonight?"

He gave a low chuckle and leaned down and brushed a kiss across her lips. "Yes, tonight."

"I'm not sure I can move."

"Um, you were doing quite nicely a while ago," he pointed out as he placed his arm around her and drew her into the curve of his body.

"Yeah, well, that's why I can't move now, thank you very much."

His expression turned serious. "No, thank *you* very much, Taylor. I owe you a wealth of thanks. I'd be the first to admit when you suggested that I father your child, I had a number of misgivings. But now since it's official that you're pregnant, I can only feel elation."

He paused for a moment and then said, "I can't wait to tell my parents."

Taylor forced her head to move to look at him. "How are you going to tell them? How will you explain the situation between us?"

"Not sure yet, but they are fully aware that I'll never marry again. They're hoping that I'll change my mind although I've told them on countless occasions that I won't."

Well, that was that, Taylor thought. What he'd said had effectively removed any hope she'd been harboring that he saw what they'd shared as something other than lust. "You could just tell them the truth, that you and I both wanted a child and so we entered into this business agreement to share one."

"Yes, I could do that but they wouldn't buy it. They would try their hand at getting us together. Unfortunately, they are die-hard romantics. They are in France now and won't be returning for a week or so. I will have thought of something by then."

Taylor was curious as to what he would come

up with but decided they were his parents and he would have to deal with them. She, on the other hand, would be busy dealing with her own family. Now it seemed Cheyenne wouldn't be the only one announcing plans of motherhood next weekend when the family got together for Marcus's graduation.

"But one thing is for certain, *chérie*," he said in a raspy tone.

Tiny flutters went off in her stomach. It always did something to her when he called her in French what was the equivalency of the word *sweetheart* in English. Although she knew it was a term of endearment that probably had no special meaning to him, she still felt something when he said it.

"And what is for certain, Dominic?"

"No matter how or why the child was conceived, they will look upon its existence like I will, as that of a special gift we've been given."

Taylor had read in a pregnancy book that emotional changes were one of the side effects. Maybe that was the reason she suddenly wanted to cry at what Dominic said. His words had touched her deeply.

"Thank you," she whispered, fighting back the tears in her eyes.

He reached out and ran the tip of his finger along the side of her jaw. "And what are you thanking me for?" he asked in a husky tone.

"For wanting this baby. For wanting it to be a part of your life, your parents' life."

"Did you think I would not, Taylor? Did you honestly assume that I would settle for anything less?"

No, she hadn't assumed that. He was living up to her expectations. Instead of answering him, she leaned forward and touched her lips to his. He then gently gathered her into his arms, took over the kiss and devoured her mouth with a hunger she was used to.

As he proceeded to kiss her senseless, she fell deeper and deeper in love with him.

Chapter 11

Vanessa Steele stared at her two younger sisters. Pregnant and unmarried—the *both* of them—they seemed happy, so she was happy for them. She knew who had fathered Taylor's child, but Cheyenne was keeping a tight lip as to who had fathered hers. The only thing Cheyenne would say was that he was someone she had met one night while doing a photo shoot in Egypt but wouldn't be seeing again. Vanessa couldn't help wondering if Cheyenne's one-night lover had been an Egyptian native or an American she'd met who, like her, had been visiting the country.

"I hope the two of you know we're going to have

to celebrate, don't you?" she finally asked. Taylor and Cheyenne were doing a sleepover at Vanessa's house. They had just watched a Tyler Perry movie that had finally come out on DVD—for the fourth time—while munching on popcorn.

Marcus's graduation had been beautiful and had brought out a lot of tears from those who recalled how it seemed just yesterday he was taking his first steps and now he was heading off to college—an Ivy League college at that, something Chance had always wanted for his son. Chance was proud of Marcus and everyone knew that if Cyndi had lived she would be proud of Marcus, as well, and more than satisfied at the fine job Chance had done in raising their son. Now Chance was married to Kylie, and had a seventeen-year-old stepdaughter named Tiffany and a baby son named Alden, who would be celebrating his first birthday soon.

Although surprised, the members of the family took both Taylor's and Cheyenne's pregnancy announcements well, and for once the cousins hadn't bothered asking a lot of questions. After all, Taylor and Cheyenne were grown women, financially secure and able to take care of themselves. But Vanessa knew everyone had to be mildly curious about the men in their lives since no one had ever met either of them.

Vanessa was more than mildly curious but knew

there was no need wasting her time on Cheyenne. Trying to get anything out of her would be like getting blood from a turnip, so she turned her concentration on Taylor.

"So, will you and Dominic Saxon have joint custody of your baby?" she asked Taylor, since she wanted to know.

Taylor shook her head. "No, I'll have full custody, but he'll get visitation rights."

Deciding to play devil's advocate, she asked, "And what if he changes his mind later and wants full custody? What will you do then?"

"It won't happen."

Vanessa raised a brow. "You seem certain of that."

Taylor shrugged. "I am. I trust Dominic to do what he said he would do."

Vanessa decided to make an observation. "You also love him, don't you?"

At first Taylor didn't say anything and then after taking a sip of her lemonade, she said, "Yes, I love him. But it doesn't matter."

"And why doesn't it matter?" Cheyenne wanted to know.

Taylor smiled at her two sisters. "Because falling in love with him wasn't part of the deal. I may never have his love but I will have his baby."

"And will that be enough for you?" Vanessa asked softly, hearing the pain in her sister's voice.

Taylor toyed with her glass a second or so before

saying, "It has to be enough, Van, because that's all I'll ever have."

Later that night Taylor couldn't get to sleep so she lay in bed and stared up at the ceiling. She couldn't help but recall the night when Dominic had dropped by her condo so he could be there when she found out whether or not she was pregnant. They had made love several times, and he had taken her to dinner later and ended up spending the night.

The following morning had been like all the others on the island when she had awakened in his arms…and to his lovemaking. He left the next morning for a business meeting in Australia. He hadn't made any promises about when he would see her again, but had promised to call to check on her and he had, practically every day. She enjoyed receiving her daily phone calls from him, although she knew he was calling more for the baby's sake than for hers.

When she had spoken to him earlier today he had mentioned that he had told his parents about the baby and they wanted to meet her. He hadn't said how he had explained their relationship and she didn't ask.

She heard her cell phone ring and glanced over at the clock. It was almost eleven. Wondering who would be calling her at this hour she got out of bed to grab the phone off the dresser. Caller ID indicated it was Dominic. Her heart jumped at the thought that he was calling her and wondered if anything was wrong, since they'd talked already that day.

"Dominic?"

"Yes, *chérie?*"

"Is anything wrong?"

She heard his soft chuckle. "No, nothing is wrong. It was only after dialing your number that I remembered there's a three-hour time difference between us. I'm back in L.A. visiting my parents."

"Oh." Earlier that day when she had spoken with him he had been in Italy. He was definitely a jet-setter, but she knew that Dominic had investment interests all over the world.

"And how are your parents?" she asked.

He gave another soft chuckle. "They're doing fine and are still walking on cloud nine at the thought of becoming grandparents. You have made them happy, Taylor. And they like the names we've picked out."

Taylor smiled. "I'm glad."

There was a slight pause and then he said, "I miss you, Taylor."

She closed her eyes at the sexiness in his voice. "I miss you, too, Dominic."

And she did, although she knew the reason she was missing him was vastly different from the reason he was missing her. She was smart enough to know that the sex between them was good, practically off the charts. Men got used to something like that. They began craving it. The reason she missed him was because she loved him and because she loved him, she enjoyed being with him whether sexual or not.

"When are you returning to D.C.?" he broke into her thoughts and asked.

"In a few days. In fact, I fly out Sunday morning."

"Call my secretary and give her your flight information. I will be at the airport to pick you up."

"You don't have to do that."

"I know, but I want to," he said smoothly in a soft voice.

"Okay then. I'll call and let her know."

Moments later after hanging up the phone she got back into bed. Her fleeting happiness was somewhat fractured by the fact that the only thing between them was sex. Good, hot, passionate sex.

And yes, of course, there was the baby.

"You're kind of antsy, aren't you, Nick? Ms. Steele's flight doesn't arrive for a full hour."

Dominic was roused from his thoughts by Ryder's observation. He glanced toward the front seat where Ryder was expertly driving the sedan toward the airport. "I didn't want to take a chance on traffic this morning," he said.

"On a Sunday morning? Who are you trying to kid? Just admit you're anxious to see the woman."

Dominic frowned. "I will admit no such thing."

"Fine, then suit yourself."

Instead of giving Ryder a response, Dominic decided to look over the papers he needed to review for a business meeting he was having in England later this week. His father was relinquishing more and more of the hotel duties to him. He didn't mind combining his father's entities with his, especially now since there would be someone they would eventually leave all their wealth, too—the Saxon heir.

It didn't take long for him to admit he was finding it hard to concentrate and tossed the papers aside. Ryder was right. He was antsy but he would never admit it. Ryder seemed to know too much as it was. But then, even as a teenager he hadn't been able to pull anything over on the man.

"So, Nick, when is the wedding?"

Now, Dominic thought, Ryder was trying to be a smart-ass. "There won't be a wedding and you know it. I've been married once."

"Yes, but Camry is gone. Besides, the two of you lacked passion."

Dominic glared at the back of the man's head. "And how would you know?"

"I have eyes. You and Camry were best friends more than anything else. You understood her whereas her parents never did."

That much was true, Dominic thought. The reason he had decided to marry her was to protect her from them. They had expected perfection and she had tried telling them time and time again that

she was only human but they wouldn't listen.
"Camry meant everything to me, Ryder."

"Yes, like I said, she was your best friend."

Dominic's eyes went cold. "She was my wife."
Ryder didn't say anything and Dominic was grateful for the man's silence.

It was short-lived.

"That baby is going to need a father, Nick."

Dominic didn't have to ask what baby he was talking about. "He or she is going to have a father."

"Yes, a part-time one. Marcello was a full-time father to you. How can you cheat your own child out of having what you had?"

Before Dominic could give Ryder a blazing retort, Ryder quickly said, "We're here. I'm going to let you out at the curb so you can be there when Ms. Steele walks off the plane since I believe that's what you want."

Dominic wouldn't argue with him about that, because that was what he wanted.

Taylor saw Dominic the minute she walked through the gate. He was standing there, tall and as handsome as any man had a right to be.

And he was waiting for her.

A shiver went up her spine when at that moment she realized the sexual chemistry between them was still there, even in the crowded airport. She continued walking toward him and he moved toward her.

The moment they were standing in front of each other, as if it had been months since he had seen her last instead of mere weeks, he pulled her into his arms and kissed her, deeply, soundly.

Moments later, knowing they were probably causing a scene, he pulled back and took her hand in his. "Come on, let's get out of here," he said gruffly.

It didn't take long for them to claim her luggage. Ryder was there with the car waiting for them the moment they stepped outside the terminal. Once Dominic had her settled in the backseat with him, ignoring Ryder, he pulled her into his arms and kissed her again, long and leisurely.

When he finally released her mouth he whispered against her moist lips, "Come to the hotel with me and let me fix you breakfast."

She took a deep breath. "You're cooking?"

He smiled. "Yes."

"Then there's no way I'll turn you down."

He gave her a soft chuckle. "I was hoping you would say that."

It was late afternoon before Taylor finally entered her apartment. After Dominic had prepared breakfast—and he'd done a good job of it, she would have to admit—they took a walk around the grounds of the hotel, which eventually led to Rock Creek Park. It was a beautiful day for a walk and she couldn't get over just how attentive Dominic had been to her.

His parents called and when he mentioned she was there, they wanted to talk to her. They were over-joyed at the thought of having a grandchild and couldn't wait to meet her. Dominic promised to fly her out to L.A. when she was free to do so.

When they returned to his suite at the hotel, they had showered together and made love. Instead of staying in bed the rest of the day as she'd figured they would do, they had dressed and gone down-stairs for brunch. Then he had taken her to the recreation room for a game of pool. He was sur-prised she knew how to play, and she had explained that she thanked her four cousins for acquiring such a skill. She had truly had fun, although he had beaten her each and every time.

They had returned to his suite and had made love again before he had brought her home. He had walked her to the door, promised to call once he arrived in London tomorrow, kissed her and then had left after seeing that she was safely inside.

Too tired to unpack her clothes, Taylor cuddled on the sofa and thought about her day with Domi-nic. Although neither had officially declared it to be so, they were lovers. They were doing all the things that lovers did.

She shook her head. This part of their relation-ship had not been planned. It just happened. Their week together on the island had done more than create a baby, it had created an unquenchable hunger for each other. She couldn't help wondering—when would the intense craving come to an end? When would he decide that he wanted another flavor of the month and move on?

She knew that because of the baby her life would always be connected to his in some way. But she also knew that she needed to prepare herself for the time when he would tell her he was no longer interested in her. In her job she was a risk taker, and one thing a risk taker knew was those risks to walk away from. She could not let Dominic break her heart, and unless she did something that was just where she was headed.

She had never been a needy person and she wasn't going to start being one now. She'd known when she had proposed the idea to Dominic that she would be sailing solo and nothing had changed. Time away from Dominic was what she needed. It was better if she got out of the situation now, on her own, before he forced her out.

With a heavy heart and a made-up mind, she pulled herself off the sofa and headed toward the bedroom to get ready for bed.

"Ms. Steele, Mr. Saxon is here to see you."

Taylor frowned. That couldn't be. Dominic had called her that morning from England and said he would be in business meetings all day. There was no way he could be back in the States.

"Mr. Saxon?" she asked, making sure she'd heard her secretary correctly.

"Yes. Mr. Franco Saxon."

Franco Saxon? Taylor pondered the name around in her mind. The only Franco Saxon she knew—or rather had heard of—was the wealthy Frenchman who'd made his millions through his shipping company. Could he be one and the same and why was he coming to see her?

"Ms. Steele?"

"Oh, yes. Please send him in."

Never in a thousand years would Taylor be prepared for the sharply dressed, gray-haired older man who walked into her office. He had such charisma and style that she immediately recognized him as someone who had to be related to Dominic. But then there were the features, so like Dominic's it was amazing. It was as if she was staring into the face of a much older Dominic. The man was tall and very handsome. It was evident the man was related to Dominic but in what capacity? Although she had yet to meet Dominic's father, she had seen pictures of him in magazines and he wasn't as old as this guy. Was this an uncle perhaps?

"Madam Steele, thank you for seeing me," he said with a deep French accent as he crossed the room to her. He leaned over and placed a kiss on the back of her hand.

"You're welcome," she said, thinking whoever he was, he was a true Frenchman.

When he straightened, a smile touched the corners of his lips. "You seem in a quandary as to who I am."

"Yes," Taylor said, studying the man's features. She would put his age in his early seventies. "It's obvious you're related to Dominic."

She saw a sudden shadow that crossed the man's green eyes, eyes that were so much like Dominic's it was uncanny. "Yes, I am related to Dominic," he said in a somewhat soft voice that dampened the smile he wore. "I am Franco Marcello Saxon, the grandfather Dominic refuses to acknowledge that he has."

Chapter 12

At first Taylor could have sworn she had heard the older man wrong, but a part of her knew deep down she'd heard him right. There was no doubt in her mind that the man standing before her was Dominic's grandfather, and since Dominic had denied having any living grandparents, she could only wonder why he refused to acknowledge the man's very existence.

"B-but why would Dominic do such a thing?" she asked, knowing the man would be able to provide her with an answer.

"It's a long story, one you have a right to know."

She wondered how he figured that. He evidently

saw the question in her eyes and said, "Because you are the woman who will give birth to my great-grandchild and more than anything, I want to be a part of its life."

Taylor wondered how he knew about the baby. Again, as if he'd known what she was thinking, he said, "My son and daughter-in-law were excited about the news and were happy to share it with me."

Taylor nodded. If that was the case, that meant he and Dominic's parents were on speaking terms. If they were then why not Dominic?

"I know you have a lot of questions, Madam Steele, and I would be honored if you joined me for dinner so I can explain things to you."

"Dinner?"

"Yes."

Taylor thought about the invitation. Regardless of whether or not he was on good terms with his grandfather, Dominic should have mentioned the man's existence to her. No matter what degree of discord subsisted between the two men, the one standing before was her baby's great-grandfather. So, she made a decision. "Yes, I would love to join you for dinner."

As soon as they entered the Marcinelli Restaurant, Taylor could tell the man by her side was used to dining in elegance. She glanced up at the vaulted ceilings with intricate carvings and bordered by rich-looking marble that seemed to blend into the stone walls. The spacious interior provided an air of sophistication and style, and the floor-to-ceiling windows and handmade pottery that sat on each table promised ambience as classy as the food the restaurant served.

They were led to a private room in the back of the restaurant and she was just as impressed with the furnishings and decor. The window looked out into a massive garden. Taylor was never one to appreciate a lot of greenery but she did so now.

Once they had been seated and their choice of wine ordered, Franco Saxon glanced over at her and smiled. "I'm glad you are joining me, Taylor. It means a lot."

She believed him, just as she believed him earlier, during the drive over, when he'd said that no matter how Dominic felt about him, he loved his grandson.

"And I appreciate the invitation to join you."

They began talking about everything but Dominic for the first half hour while waiting for their food to arrive. He told her that his health hadn't been the best lately, but he was getting better and that his travels to the United States were infrequent. She discovered his love of classical music as well as his opposition to anything that restricted world trade. That was understandable considering he had made his millions in the import and export business.

"I can see why my grandson has fallen in love with you, Taylor."

Taylor froze with the glass of apple juice halfway to her lips. She wasn't sure what to say, since she didn't have a clue just what Dominic had told his parents about her. So to play it safe, she said something she knew wasn't a lie. "And I love Dominic just as deeply."

She leaned back in her chair. "So, please, share with me why there is animosity between you and Dominic."

Over dinner she listened while he told her with deep regret and sorrow in his voice how he tried to control his son's life by choosing the woman for him to marry—a woman who would increase the Saxons' wealth when the two families joined. Instead, while attending school here in the States, Marcello met and fell in love with Megan. Franco had opposed the marriage, threatened to disown his son if he didn't do what he wanted. In the end, Marcello chose love.

For the next twenty years Marcello and his father had very little contact. Franco explained that they were both stubborn men, but that within the last three years he and Marcello had put the past behind them. However, Dominic refused to do so. He just couldn't get over the fact that Franco had turned his back on Marcello for marrying his mother.

Franco admitted he had been wrong and that he had made a grave mistake, especially upon seeing how happy Marcello was. And he totally liked

Megan and couldn't imagine any woman more right
for his son. If he had it to do all over again, he
would give his blessings to the couple in a heartbeat.
But he hadn't and not doing so had eventually lost
him his grandson's love.

"Have you tried talking to Dominic?" Taylor
couldn't help but ask.

"Yes, but he refuses to discuss anything with
me. Dominic refuses to acknowledge my very existence. And that's why I wanted to talk to you. I
hope that you will find it in your heart to allow me
to be a part of my great-grandchild's life. I hope
you won't deny me that."

Taylor shook her head. "Of course I won't, and
I can't see Dominic denying it, either."

"Forgive me for saying so, but I can see him
denying it. Like I said, I am not one of my grandson's favorite people, but I love him and will do
anything I can for him."

"And now that Dominic sees how his parents
have forgiven you, that doesn't change his feelings
about you?"

"No. It seems he has more stubbornness than me
and his father put together. And he is fiercely loyal
to those he loves and he loves his parents deeply.
He knows how much I've hurt them and won't forgive me for doing so."

The older man paused for a second and then he
said, "Dominic refuses to acknowledge his place

as my rightful heir, but I'm naming him in my business papers anyway. However, I want to meet with my attorney and make provisions for my great-grandchild to be included, as well, but wanted to meet with you to make sure you are fine with that."

Taylor stared at him. Being a wealth and asset manager, she had a pretty good idea just how wealthy Franco Saxon was, and he was sitting there letting her know that he was thinking of her child and his place in its life. "Yes, I'm fine with it. In fact, your generosity overwhelms me and I don't know what to say."

"Say that as long as I have breath in my body that I will be a part of my great-grandchild's life. I messed up with my grandson but I don't want to mess up with my great-grandchild."

Taylor heard the trembling in the man's voice. He truly did love Dominic and was sorry for what he'd done all those years ago. Why couldn't Dominic see that? She reached across the table and took the man's hand into hers. "I make you that promise. You are the only great-grandparent my child will have and I am honored that you will be—want to be—a part of his or her life."

She could tell her words had touched Franco, and he quickly glanced away so she wouldn't see the tears in his eyes. Moments later, he looked back at her and said in a soft, appreciative voice, "Thank you, Taylor. You have brought joy to an old man's heart."

* * *

Later that night as Taylor slid under her bedcovers she couldn't help but recall her dinner conversations with Franco. He was a proud man, yet he had humbled himself and admitted to the mistakes he'd made years ago by alienating his son and grandson. She had made Franco a promise tonight, one she intended to keep. Besides, she liked him. He indicated he would be leaving D.C. in the morning but had given her his business card and had invited her to come visit him in France. Before they had parted ways she had made another promise to him that she would.

She almost jumped when her phone rang. She hadn't been sure Dominic would call and hoped it was him. She wouldn't mention anything about her dinner meeting with his grandfather until she saw him. She wanted to be face-to-face with him when she did so. For now, she just wanted to hear his voice.

She leaned up and reached over and picked up her cell phone off the nightstand. "Hello."

"Did I wake you?"

She smiled. "No, I'm in bed but I hadn't gone to sleep yet. Are you still in London?"

"No, I'm on a plane returning to the States."

She felt a gentle tug of joy in her stomach. He was on his way home. "You're going to Los Angeles?"

"No, I'm headed straight for where you are," he said softly. "By the time you awake in the morning I should have landed. I miss you."

She felt another pull in her stomach. "And I miss you, too."

"Will it be okay for me to come straight there from the airport?" he asked.

A grin touched her lips. "Yes, most certainly."

She heard his soft chuckle. "In that case, I'm going to let you go so you can get your rest. Trust me when I say that you're going to need it."

She clearly understood his underlying hint and countered, "I encourage you to take a few catnaps on the plane as you're going to need your rest, as well."

After Dominic ended his conversation with Taylor he leaned back in the leather seat and closed his eyes. God, he missed her. For the past week he could barely concentrate on business without thinking about her. The meetings with his business associates had been intense, and with a heaping amount of sexual frustration thrown into the mix, negotiations at times had gotten downright heated. In the end, he had closed the deal he had wanted and his mission had been accomplished. Now he could set his mind and sights to other things.

Like finally acknowledging he had fallen in love with Taylor.

It had been bound to happen at some point, he thought. The week on that island had been no joke. Since then he had been trying to convince himself his attraction to her was only sexual, and that since

Camry he had enjoyed a number of women's company. But he'd known this thing with Taylor went deeper.

He would never forget the exact moment he'd realized just how he felt. It was the last time they had made love. After experiencing what he considered as the best orgasm of his life, he had lain beside her, held her in his arms when suddenly, his mind and body had begun reeling before experiencing a feeling of having been punched in the gut by one of those wrestlers Ryder liked watching on television.

Dominic had been tempted to tell her then, but had decided to wait, to think more about his feelings and to give himself time to contemplate hers, as well as to set up a plan of action if he discovered she wasn't feeling the same way he was. He knew one of the things that made his parents' marriage special was their love for each other. Theirs was not a one-sided love match.

And he wanted the same thing for him and Taylor. If she didn't love him now, by the time he was through with her, she would. He loved her and she was going to have his baby. He was a very lucky man, a man very much in love with the mother of his child. Now his goal was to do whatever it took to make sure Taylor loved him, as well. His mission was to win her heart.

Taylor had gotten a good night's rest, grateful it was Saturday and that she wouldn't have to go into the office. She glanced at the clock. It wasn't quite seven but she'd hoped Dominic would have arrived by now.

She had gotten up at the crack of dawn and although she hadn't bothered changing out of her nightclothes, she had washed her face, brushed her teeth and tried making her hair look decent.

If it wasn't so early in the morning she would call Cheyenne to check on her. They had talked a few nights ago and her sister was doing better with her pregnancy. The morning sickness was easing up somewhat with Cheyenne whereas so far Taylor hadn't experienced one day of her stomach feeling queasy.

Taylor's heart leaped in her chest when she heard the sound of the doorbell. She inhaled deeply as she crossed the room to answer it. The moment she opened the door to find Dominic standing there, immaculate as ever, simply breathtaking, whatever emotions she had been feeling before were nothing compared to what she was feeling now. Whether he loved her or not didn't matter. She truly loved him.

"Taylor…"

And then she realized that he had taken a step into the room, closed and locked the door behind him and had whispered her name just seconds before pulling her into his arms. The moment their mouths touched she felt it all the way to the bone, and she put her heart, body and soul into their kiss.

And when she felt herself being swept up into his

arms, her body began aching with need, as he headed for the bedroom. She was so consumed with wanting and desire she barely realized the moment he had placed her on the bed, joined her there and began removing their clothes.

But she was fully aware of when he moved his body over hers and began kissing her again with a hunger that sent blood gushing through her veins. And when she felt the thickness of his erection, poised against her feminine core, she wanted him with a degree that she never wanted him before. And knowing that he wanted her, as well, that he was barely holding back and that possibly the moment he entered her he would explode, had her tense on the verge of reaching an orgasm just that quick. They would savor the next one. Now what the two of them needed, what they wanted was immediate satisfaction.

He glanced down at her, opened his mouth to say something, but whatever he was about to say was lost when she lifted her hips and forced him to enter her. He threw his head back and growled out her name the exact moment he thrust forward, going deep, spilling inside her with an orgasm of gigantic magnitude. She came the moment she felt his hot release and wrapped her legs around him, locking him to her.

Bringing his head down, she pressed her mouth to his as all the passion and love she felt flowed through her, began overtaking her. Her moans of pleasure mingled with his and their bodies began shuddering and this was one magical moment that she didn't ever want to end.

"Who gave you this, Taylor?"

Upon hearing Dominic's voice it took her a moment to muster up enough strength to open her eyes. Their lovemaking sessions always left her weak as water from nearly drowning in passion.

She brought him into focus. He was sitting on the edge of the bed holding something in his hand. She blinked to bring him into focus again and saw it was the business card his grandfather had given her. She inhaled sharply, much preferring to have waited before having this conversation with him, but it seemed that that wouldn't be the case.

"Taylor?"

He had turned and was looking at her intensely. In other words, he was frowning. She slowly pulled up in bed, mindful of the fact that like him, she was stark naked.

"Your grandfather gave it to me."

The look he gave her was one as if he'd been slapped and then he said harshly, "That's impossible because I don't have a grandfather."

She rolled her eyes. "At least not one you want to claim. You should have told me about him, Dominic. I had a right to know."

He stood and stared down at her. "The only rights
you have regarding me are the ones I give you,
Taylor, and an association with Franco Saxon isn't
one of them. The man means nothing to me."

She glared at Dominic. "He might not mean anything to you, but he is my child's great-grandfather."

"No, he is not!"

"Yes, he is," she said, struggling to keep her voice
calm. "Don't you think it's time for you to forgive
him and move on?"

Dominic looked livid. He reached out and gripped
her wrist and brought her closer to him. "No. And I
don't want him to be a part of my child's life."

"And I intend for him to be a part of it, Dominic.
I made him a promise."

He let go of her hand. "How much did he offer,
Taylor?"

"What are you talking about?"

"I know the man. For years he's been trying to
win me over with his money, with offers of business
deals, the naming of me as his heir, ownership of
his shipping company...so I'm sure he offered you
something. What was it?" he demanded.

Taylor didn't like the sound of Dominic's raised
voice, nor of his insinuations. "Are you saying that
you believe I made a promise to your grandfather
because of some money deal?"

"Didn't you? Are you saying he didn't agree to

acknowledge our unborn child as his heir if you went along with him?"

His words made Taylor furious. "It wasn't like that at all, Dominic. Franco is a man who loves you and who already loves his great-grandchild. He merely wants to be a part of our baby's life and I can see no reason why he should not."

"Well, I do and I won't have it."

She leaned forward and placed her hands on her naked hips. "I don't care what you won't have so get over it. I will not break my promise to him."

"And what about your loyalty to me?"

Taylor figured that now was not the time to tell Dominic that not only did he have her loyalty but that he also had her love, but that this was one issue she could not, would not agree with him on. "I am loyal to you, Dominic, however, I will not deny my child the right to know its great-grandparent."

The room got quiet, and the tension surrounding them was almost unbearable. Then Dominic spoke as he began picking up his clothes off the floor. "Then it seems we have nothing more to discuss, Taylor."

He turned his back on her and went into the bathroom and closed the door. He reappeared in the room a short while later fully dressed. He came over to the bed, stood over her and glared down at her. His face was tight, his features still intense. "I'm leaving."

"Fine, and once you realize just how unfair you're being, please call me."

He face darkened. "I will call occasionally for no other reason than to check on my child. Otherwise, Taylor, our association is over."

Taylor fought back the tears in her eyes. "If that's the way you want things, Dominic, then that's the way they will be."

He stared down at her for a few more minutes and then without saying anything else, he turned and walked out of her condo.

It was later that day before Taylor was able to get out of bed, and only then because she knew she needed to eat something. She had to take care of the life growing inside her—the life Dominic had placed there.

As she began moving around her apartment, she couldn't put out of her mind the words Dominic had spoken. Did he hate his grandfather that much? Okay, she could imagine how he must have felt as a child growing up to discover the rift that existed between his parents and his grandfather, but if his parents could forgive the man, then why couldn't he?

"Because he is so damn stubborn," Taylor muttered as she sat down to eat a bowl of cereal and milk. "Okay, so I won't be at his beck and call anymore," she said to the walls, sneering. "It will be his loss. I should not have been at his beck and call anyway. The only thing between us was lust...at least on his end." She knew for her it was more. It was love.

After breakfast she decided to go for a walk. She had to leave the apartment for a while. And later she would take in a movie. She needed to keep her mind occupied so Dominic wouldn't consume so much of it. He'd made his feelings clear and there was nothing left for her to do but accept it and move on.

And she would. He'd given her no choice.

Chapter 13

Two weeks later, Dominic was standing at the window in his New York office, staring down at the people below. They were moving rather quickly along the sidewalk, and he thought about just how fast their lives seemed to be moving. But for him it appeared that his had come to a complete standstill.

And all because of Taylor.

He inhaled deeply. He hadn't realized just how much he loved her until he'd had to do without her. He had called her twice and their conversations had been brief. He had asked how she was doing, she had said fine, and then she had ended the call. He had said some harsh words to her that day, words he now wished he could take back.

Taylor was who she was and he couldn't expect her to have a beef with his grandfather just because he had one. She was not that type of woman. She had a mind of her own, she thought for herself. He would not have wanted her any other way.

And he did want her. Damn, he also loved her but he had been willing to turn his back on that love and let his intense stubbornness rule his mind and common sense. But it hadn't been able to eradicate what was in his heart.

"Mr. Saxon, your mother is here to see you."

He turned at the sound of his secretary's voice on the intercom. As much as he loved his mother she was the last person he wanted to see right now. She had gotten upset with him when he had told her about the argument he'd had with Taylor. His mother had called him, among other things, pigheaded.

"Mr. Saxon?"

"Yes, Liza, please send her in."

The door opened and his mother walked in, beautiful as ever, but she was frowning. She retained that frown as she crossed the room and came to a stop in front of him.

"Okay, Nicky, you have sulked long enough. By now I had hoped you would have come to your senses. I want to know just what you're going to do to get the mother of my grandchild back?"

Her question, Dominic thought, was simple enough, but to be completely honest, he didn't have a clue. For all he knew, Taylor might not want to be gotten back. The last two times they had talked she didn't seem inclined to have anything more to do with him.

"It's not going to be easy," he said quietly.

Megan placed a hand on his arm and he couldn't help noticing her eyes had softened somewhat and her frown was gone. "Do you want her back?"

"Yes, I want her back," he didn't hesitate to say. "Besides you, she is the most remarkable woman I know."

A smile touched Megan Saxon's lips. "You love her, don't you?"

Dominic met his mother's inquisitive but gentle stare and said, "Yes, I love her."

"Then you're going to have to do whatever it takes to win her heart and convince her that you were wrong and that you love her," Megan said in a soft voice. "Let love guide you to do the right thing. And when you get things straightened out, let me and your father know. We still want to meet her. Regardless of your relationship, she is the mother of our grandchild." She glanced at her watch. "I have to go, our private plane is waiting."

He lifted a brow. "And where are you and Dad off to now?"

"Paris. It's your grandfather's seventieth birthday and we're flying in for the birthday celebration planned for tomorrow night. I'll talk to you when I get back."

After his mother had left, Dominic sat at his desk while he planned his strategy to win back Taylor. Moments later after taking a deep breath he picked up the phone and punched in the phone number to her cell phone. He leaned back in the chair, waiting for her to answer.

Instead, another voice came on the line that said, *"I am sorry, but at the customer's request, this number has been changed to a nonpublished number."* Then there was a sharp click in his ear.

He slowly hung up the phone. Taylor had changed her number? Not to be denied the right to speak with her, he then pulled her business card from his desk to try reaching her at the office. Her secretary's cheery voice came on the line. "Good afternoon, Assets of Steele. May I help you?"

"Yes, this is Dominic Saxon and I would like to speak with Ms. Steele, please."

"I'm sorry, Mr. Saxon, but Ms. Steele is out of town."

"I see," he said, somewhat disappointed. "Is she visiting her family in North Carolina?"

"No, sir, she is out of the country."

Dominic frowned as he stood from his seat. "Out of the country? Where did she go?" he asked, as if he had a right to know.

There was a pause, and then as if the secretary decided that maybe he did, she said, "She's in France."

He lifted a brow. "France?"

"Yes, sir, Paris, France. If this is an emergency, she has asked that I refer those calls to…"

Whatever the woman was saying was lost on Dominic. Taylor had gone to France and he had an idea as to why and who she had gone to see. "Well, thanks for the information," he said, interrupting whatever it was Taylor's secretary was saying. He quickly hung up and then pressed a button.

"Yes, Mr. Saxon?"

"Liza, I'd like you to contact Martin and tell him to have the plane ready to fly me out in a few hours."

"Yes sir, and the destination?"

"Paris, France."

"Are you feeling better today, dear?"

Taylor smiled at Franco Saxon as she came down the steps to join him on the terrace for a midmorning meal. "Yes, a lot better."

She had arrived at the Saxon Estates yesterday after having endured the lengthy plane flight across the Atlantic. Evidently something she had eaten had not agreed with her and in addition to jet lag, she had endured an upset stomach. After a good night's sleep she was now feeling fine.

She glanced around as she took her seat across from Dominic's grandfather. The Saxon family home was simply beautiful. According to Franco, it had been in the Saxon family since the late eighteen hundreds and was the place where all the Saxons, including Marcello, were born. The palace-style structure was composed of several reception rooms. Numerous bedroom suites with private baths and dressing rooms, game rooms, spa, gym, two swimming pools and a beautiful kitchen and dining room. It was a beautiful day and the sun was shining bright in the sky.

"I received a call this morning from Marcello and Megan. They are on their way and should be arriving later today," Franco said, intruding into Taylor's thoughts.

She nodded as butterflies went off in her stomach at the thought of meeting Dominic's parents. She couldn't help wondering what he'd told them about their now-defunct relationship.

She had been surprised when she had received a call from Franco inviting her to his birthday gala. Since she hadn't been sure if Dominic was still in the D.C. area or had returned to New York, she hadn't wanted to run the risk of a chance meeting with him—especially while her heart was still hurting—and had jumped at the opportunity to leave the city for a few days. The last thing she had to worry about was running into Dominic here.

The one thing she was certain about was that she truly liked Dominic's grandfather. She believed that deep in Franco's heart he knew that he had made a mistake in the way he had handled his son's love for an American woman, a mistake that had cost him the love of his grandson. And from their argument the last time she and Dominic were together, she wasn't sure if he would ever forgive his grandfather. Dominic took being stubborn to all-new heights.

After their meal, she and Franco went into one of the game rooms to play checkers, something the older man seemed to enjoy. She was glad that her cousin Sebastian had taught her how to play years ago.

They had just ended one game and had started on another when one of Franco's servants approached to let him know that Marcello and Megan had arrived.

"Why, you're simply beautiful, just as Dominic said," his mother exclaimed, smiling at her.

Taylor wondered if Dominic had actually said that, or whether his mother was just being kind. Either way she decided to take the compliment. "Thank you."

They were standing together in the receiving line, greeting the guests arriving at Franco's party. Franco had asked her to be there and as far as she knew, no one seemed to question it. When introducing her, he merely said that she was a close friend of his grandson. Considering how things were between her and Dominic, Taylor thought that was really stretching it a bit.

"We certainly have a crowd here tonight."

Megan's words broke into Taylor's thoughts. "Yes, there are a number of people here, but everything is beautiful. And speaking of beautiful…"

The first thing Taylor had thought when she'd seen Megan Saxon was that any picture she'd seen of her in a magazine hadn't done her justice. She was a beautiful woman and it only took a few seconds in the Saxons' company to know that Marcello simply adored his wife. Dominic had once commented on what a loving relationship his mother and father had. Now she saw firsthand just how true that statement had been.

"And your outfit is divine. That color looks good on you," the older woman added.

Suddenly a deep appreciation for Megan Saxon blossomed to life inside her. That compliment meant a lot coming from a person who was considered an expert on fashion. But that wasn't the only reason she liked Dominic's mother so much. From the moment Franco had introduced them earlier that day, she had felt a connection. Maybe it had something to do with the fact that Megan was the woman who had given birth to the man who had captured Taylor's heart, or possibly the fact that Taylor was carrying inside her this woman's grandchild. Whatever the reason, she felt an accord with Megan, a closeness to her that she couldn't explain and

wouldn't bother dissecting. It was enough that
knowing how Dominic felt about his grandfather,
they didn't have a problem with her being here or
feel she was being disloyal to Dominic for doing so.

"Yes, I can see why Nicky loves you so much."

A flicker of panic went off inside Taylor. She
knew Megan's statement was based on assumption
rather than fact. Would it be the proper thing to do
to correct her, let her know she was not the object
of Dominic's affections?

At that moment it seemed the entire room got
quiet and as Taylor glanced around to see what had
everyone's attention, she heard Marcello Saxon,
who was standing beside Megan, say, "Look who's
here, Megan. I never thought I would live to see the
day." Deep emotion was in the man's voice.

Taylor turned her head to see what the Saxons
were talking about and sharpened her gaze to look
at the single guest who had just entered and the
curious onlookers surrounding him.

She heard Franco's sharp intake of breath at the
same moment the crowd dispersed somewhat and
Dominic stood there, a younger version of both
Franco and Marcello, but definitely more of Franco.
There was no doubt in anyone's mind who he was
and his relationship to the honoree.

Unease flickered inside her the moment her and
Dominic's gazes connected and he began walking
in her direction. "My prayers have been answered,"

she heard Franco say in a voice so low she barely heard him.

She continued to hold Dominic's gaze as she studied his face. How did he feel about her being there, especially after their last conversation? Was he questioning what right she had to be standing with his family? But more important, was his presence an indication that he was willing to make peace with his grandfather at last?

She knew only Dominic held the answer to both of those questions and as she studied his features, she found nothing that would give her a clue as to what he was thinking.

Deciding she was making herself a nervous wreck, she just stood there as he came closer, as his gazed pinned her to the spot. She didn't have to force herself to hold his gaze. He was a man who deserved attention and he was definitely getting it.

The room was still quiet. It seemed that someone had even ordered the band to stop playing. Then she recalled all the people she had been introduced to that night. They were all friends and acquaintances of Franco, people who probably knew of the long-standing dissent between him and his grandson. Like her, they were waiting to see why Dominic was there, and hoping and praying that since it was Franco's birthday, Dominic's presence was a positive and not a negative.

He finally reached them and respectfully, he gave

his grandfather his full attention. Speaking in fluent French, he said, "Happy birthday, Grandfather. And I hope my presence here tonight is taken as an indication that I want to put the past behind me and move forward."

He then glanced at Taylor and the look she saw in his eyes made her heart beat faster. He hadn't touched her, had yet to acknowledge her presence, but the look in his eyes was the look he always had in them for her. Dominic then turned back to his grandfather, and, still speaking in fluent French, said, "And thanks for the safekeeping of the woman who has my heart."

His words would have meant everything to her if she hadn't known he was merely saying them for show, she thought miserably. He couldn't very well have said, *"Thanks for the safekeeping of the woman who's having my baby,"* could he? At least not in front of an audience of about three hundred individuals.

She heard Franco's emotional response. "Thank you for coming, grandson of my heart. We must talk later."

Dominic nodded. And then he came to stand in front of her and she forced her heart rate to slow down. Instead of saying anything, he took her hand and lifted it up to his lips and gazed deep into her eyes. "You look beautiful tonight," he said in English and it was then she remembered that he didn't know she spoke French and decided to answer him in his grandfather's native tongue to make him aware that she had understood what he had said to Franco.

"And you're looking rather handsome yourself," she responded. She saw the surprised lifting of his brow and then the smile that touched the corners of his lips.

Instead of saying anything else, he moved on to his parents. She saw what amounted to tears in his parents' eyes and she knew for Marcello and Megan, Dominic's presence here tonight was the beginning to putting an end to the discord that had begun when they had been bold enough to fall in love.

Then Dominic was back in front of her, reaching for her hand. "Will you dance with me Taylor?"

She was about to tell him that there was no music, when suddenly as if on cue, the orchestra started up again. "Yes, I'll dance with you," she responded, and she then found herself led out onto the dance floor.

He's only being kind to me because of the baby, she reminded herself when he took her into his arms. But still, she couldn't stop the gratitude she felt in knowing that he had taken the first steps in putting animosity behind him and making up with his grandfather.

The moment Dominic pulled her into his arms, her body seemed to recognize him and melted against him. And she couldn't help but take note that although he was holding her decently, he was doing so with such familiarity that made anyone who was watching aware that they were either past or present lovers.

"I miss you," he whispered in her ear.

Those three words lifted her spirit, revived her hope. She was about to respond by telling him that she had missed him, as well, but stopped herself from doing so. She and Dominic needed to reach an understanding. It would be better if they stuck with their original plan. Once she got pregnant, they were to go back to executing business as usual.

So she didn't say anything, didn't bother acknowledging his words. Instead she kept her head resting on his chest with her eyes closed as she remembered better times between them: the seven days they had been on the island and how she had felt a connection to him in a way that even now heated her blood just thinking about it.

"Come on, let's go for a walk outside," he leaned down and whispered against her ear. It was then she noted the music had stopped playing. She pulled back and nodded. And then she allowed him to lead her out of the doors that led to the terrace.

For a few moments they didn't say anything as they walked side by side along the stone walkway. It was a beautiful night in May. Stars were dotting the sky and a half moon sat in their wake.

"Why did you change your phone number, Taylor?"

His question intruded into her thoughts. "I thought, considering everything, it was best. You had my business number if you needed to contact me."

He nodded. "And how have you been doing?" he asked in a tone that let her know he truly wanted to know.

"Fine."

"And the baby?"

"Fine, as well. I went to the doctor last week and she said everything appears as it should be."

"Good." Then he stopped walking and turned to her. "I want to apologize for all those things I said that night to you. I had no right."

No, he hadn't. She shrugged. "It doesn't matter."

"Yes, it does. In order for us to move forward I think it does matter. I've been doing a lot of thinking over the past two weeks, and you were right. I can't hold a grudge against my grandfather forever. He's done more than enough over the years to let me know that he regretted the position he'd taken with my parents. I guess it was so easy just to dislike him rather than admit how much I actually wanted him in my life."

He didn't say anything for a moment and then, "I can vividly recall a kidnapping attempt when I was fourteen."

Ignoring her flinch of surprise, he continued.

"Luckily it wasn't successful but soon after that Ryder appeared on the scene as my bodyguard and he's been with me ever since, nearly twenty years now. It wasn't until I was in college that I learned that Ryder had been sent by my grandfather to protect me, keep me out of harm's way. Even then, I was too stubborn to admit that my grandfather had to have cared about me to do such a thing. I've suddenly come to realize that life is too short and that we should cherish each day that comes, along with the people who are there. My grandfather is seventy today, so many years have been wasted already and I don't want to waste others. You were right. I shouldn't deny him the chance to know his great-grandchild…or the woman whom his grandson has fallen in love with."

Taylor went completely still with his words. "What did you say?" she whispered softly, absolutely sure she hadn't heard him correctly.

"I said," he muttered, leaning down closer to her lips, "that I don't want to deny my grandfather the chance of getting to know his great-grandchild, or you, the woman I've fallen in love with. And I do love you, *chérie.* I've known it for some time now. I just realized how much over the past two weeks."

Taylor inhaled sharply, held the air in her lungs and then released it to ask, "Are you sure?"

He smiled. "That's the one thing I am sure about. What I'm not sure about is how you feel about me."

She took a step closer to him. Reached up and

cupped his face in her hands while tears glittered in her eyes. "I love you, too, Dominic. I thought I only wanted your baby, but then I discovered I wanted your love, as well."

"Now you have both. But there is one more thing I want you to have. My name."

Reaching into the back pocket of his pants, he pulled out a white velvet box. Her eyes widened and she stared in amazement at the huge diamond ring.

"Pretty soon your stomach will grow, declaring to all the degree of my passion for you. I want them to know the depth of my love for you, as well."

He took the ring out the box and slid it onto her finger. "Will you marry me, Taylor?" he asked softly.

More tears came into her eyes and complete happiness filled her entire being. "Oh, yes, I will marry you," she said, smiling through her tears.

"Tomorrow."

She blinked. "Tomorrow?"

"Yes, I want us to marry tomorrow. We can arrange a reception later in the States with our families, but I don't want to leave Paris without binding you to me. I love you so much I can't imagine my life not joined with yours. Will you let me marry you tomorrow?"

"Yes."

He smiled before lowering his mouth to hers. The moment their lips touched she knew in her heart that this would be the start of the rest of their lives.

Epilogue

June

Tears formed in Taylor's eyes as she stood as a bridesmaid and watched her sister join in marriage with the man she loved. She could recall when Cameron had begun showing an interest in Vanessa and how Vanessa had refused to even consider him as a man she wanted to love.

But today she was pledging her life to him and Vanessa's eyes were filled with so much love that Taylor could actually feel it. Her gaze left Vanessa and Cameron momentarily to search out a man sitting in the audience.

Her husband.

She and Dominic's eyes connected and she knew like her, he was remembering that day in Paris when they had done what Vanessa and Cameron were doing now. Franco had been more than happy to make the arrangements and Dominic's parents had stood in as witnesses, and Dominic's best friend, Matt, had flown in to be his best man.

That night he had whisked her away to his island off the Normandy coast where they had spent the next three nights more in bed than out. They had returned to Paris and spent a few more days with Dominic's parents and grandfather. Dominic and Franco talked, spent a lot of time together as they tried to accept what happened years ago as history and move on. A wedding reception was planned for them here in Charlotte in August and she was very happy about it. They had also made plans to return to Latois again in a couple of years. They wanted at least two more children and thought the island had proven to be the perfect place for future Saxons to be conceived.

Taylor then glanced sideways at Cheyenne, who at the last minute had to have her bridesmaid dress altered due to her already protruding stomach. According to Cheyenne the doctor suspected she was having twins, possibly triplets, which was the reason at three months she looked like she was actually six. A sonogram was scheduled for next

week. As far as they knew, there was no record of
twins ever being born in the Steele family, so everyone was wondering about the man who had fathered
Cheyenne's child. Was there a history of multiple
births in his? Cheyenne still refused to even give the
man's name.

"I now pronounce you man and wife."

Her gaze returned to Cameron and Vanessa just
as Cameron kissed his bride, finally claiming her as
his. Vanessa Steele was now Vanessa Steele Cody.

"It was a beautiful wedding, wasn't it?" she asked
Dominic later as she lay curled up in his arms in bed.
One of the wedding gifts Dominic had bought for
her was this beautiful home not far from where
Morgan and Lena lived. It would be available for
them to use whenever she wanted to visit home.

"Yes, but nothing is more beautiful than a Paris
wedding," he said, leaning down and kissing her
lips. "You looked simply stunning that day."

Taylor had to agree. Thanks to the Megan Saxon
original she'd been wearing. His mother was simply
incredible. Megan had made a few phone calls and
the dress had been delivered to the Saxon Estate just
hours before the wedding. Franco had hired a photographer and numerous photos were taken. Every
time she glanced through the wedding album she
was reminded of the day that she married the man
who now meant the world to her.

"And you looked handsome yourself," she added. And he had. "I love you," she whispered, doubting she would ever tire of telling him that.

"And I love you and I plan on spending the rest of my life showing you how much."

And then he spoke those same words to her in French as she stared into the depths of his green eyes. And she knew that she would spend the rest of her life showing him how much she loved him, as well.

USA TODAY Bestselling Author

BRENDA JACKSON

invites you to discover the always sexy and
always satisfying Madaris Men.

Experience where it all started…

Tonight and Forever
December 2007

Whispered Promises
January 2008

Eternally Yours
February 2008

One Special Moment
March 2008

ARABESQUE®

www.kimanipress.com   KPBJREISSUES08

Book #1 in

THE THREE MRS. FOSTERS

THIS TIME FOR GOOD

FAVORITE AUTHOR

CARMEN GREEN

About to lose her family business because of her late
husband's polygamy, Alexandria accepts Hunter's help.
But she's not letting any man run her life—
not even one who sets her senses aflame.

"Ms. Green sweeps the reader away on the lush carpet
of reality-grounded romantic fantasy."
—*Romantic Times BOOKreviews* on *Commitments*

***Coming the first week of May
wherever books are sold.***

KIMANI™
ROMANCE

www.kimanipress.com   KPCG0650508

Down and out...but not really

Indiscriminate Attraction

ESSENCE BESTSELLING AUTHOR
LINDA HUDSON-SMITH

Searching the streets and homeless shelters for his missing
twin, shabbily disguised Chad Kingston accepts volunteer
Laylah Versailles's help. Luscious Laylah's determination
to turn "down-and-out" Chad's life around has a heated
effect on him. But Chad's never trusted women—
and Laylah has secrets.

"Hudson-Smith does an outstanding job…
A truly inspiring novel!"
—*Romantic Times BOOKreviews* on *Secrets & Silence*

*Coming the first week of May
wherever books are sold.*

KIMANI™
ROMANCE

www.kimanipress.com

her kind of *Man*

Favorite author

PAMELA YAYE

As a gawky teen, Makayla Stevens yearned for
Kenyon Blake. Now he's the uncle of one of her students,
and wants to get better acquainted with Makayla.
The reality is even hotter than her teenage fantasies.
But their involvement could damage her career…
and her peace of mind.

"*Other People's Business*…is a fun and lighthearted story…
an entertaining novel."
—*Romantic Times BOOKreviews* on
Pamela Yaye's debut novel

*Coming the first week of May
wherever books are sold.*

KIMANI™
ROMANCE

"Byrd proves once again that she's
a wonderful storyteller."
—*Romantic Times BOOKreviews*
on *The Beautiful Ones*

ACCLAIMED AUTHOR

ADRIANNE
byrd

controversy

Michael Adams is no murderer—even if she did
joke about killing her ex-husband after their nasty
divorce. Now she has to prove to investigating
detective Kyson Dekker that she's innocent.
Of course, it doesn't help that he's so distractingly
gorgeous that Michael can't think straight....

***Coming the first week of May
wherever books are sold.***

ARABESQUE®

www.kimanipress.com

KPAB1000508

Her dreams of love came true...twice.

ESSENCE BESTSELLING AUTHOR

DONNA HILL

Charade

Betrayed by Miles Bennett, the first man she'd let into her heart, Tyler Ellington flees to Savannah where she falls for photographer Sterling Grey. Sterling is everything Miles is not...humorous, compassionate, honest. But when she returns to New York, Tyler is yet again swayed by Miles's apologies and passion. Now torn between two men, she must decide which love is the real thing.

"A lighthearted comedy, rich in flavor and unpredictable in story, *Divas, Inc.* proves how limitless this author's talent is."
—*Romantic Times BOOKreviews*

*Coming the first week of May
wherever books are sold.*

ARABESQUE®

www.kimanipress.com

KPDHI010508

*Overcoming the past to enjoy
the present can be difficult...*

YOLONDA TONETTE SANDERS

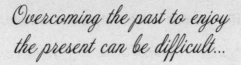

Secrets of a *Sinner*

After years of doing whatever was necessary to survive,
Natalie Coleman finally feels her life is getting back on
track. Returning to the home she ran from years ago, she
confronts the painful events of her past. As old wounds
heal, Natalie realizes God has led her home to show her
that every sinner can be saved, every life redeemed.

"Need a little good news in your novels? Look no further."
—*Essence* on *Soul Matters*

Coming the first week of May wherever books are sold.

www.kimanipress.com   KPYTS1320508